The Fourth Angel

OTHER BOOKS BY JOHN RECHY

City of Night
Numbers
This Day's Death
The Vampires

The Fourth Angel

JOHN RECHY

GROVE PRESS
NEW YORK
Seaver Books

Originally published as A Richard Seaver Book/The Viking Press
in 1973 by The Viking Press, Inc.
First paperback edition 1983

Printed in the United States of America

Library of Congress Cataloging-in-Publication Data

Rechy, John.
The fourth angel.
I. Title
PS3568.E28F6   1983   813'.54   83-10863
ISBN 0-8021-5197-3 (pbk.)

Grove Press
841 Broadway
New York, NY 10003

For the Memory of My Mother,
of Luis,
of Richard Miller,

and for Olga and Floriano

'Then they followed
Where the vision led,
And saw their sleeping child
Among tigers wild.'
William Blake

I

Shell lies on the resurrected grass of Memorial Park. His legs straddling her, Cob's body grinds over hers. But she's not looking at him—she stares at the sheet of azure sky, determined that it hold her total attention. And although his thighs press fiercely against her torso and one of his hands draws her face roughly to him from the neck, Cob doesn't look at her either. Instead, locked behind large, deep-purple sunglasses, his dark, dark eyes search the park. Both sixteen, they thrust coldly against each other as if engaged in a deadly struggle.

'Do you see him yet?' she asks him, her gaze still nailed to the sky.

'No, man, not yet,' he answers curtly.

Shell's hair is long, very long, brown, streaked blond; dark-lashed, her eyes are leonine yellow. Conveying premature scorn and too large for the rest of her chiseled features, her lips incongruously complete her stark beauty.

She twists her full but slender body under the weight of Cob's. 'Cool it, man; you're fucking hurting me,' she says. Her voice is husky beyond her years.

Cob pushes his hair, long to his shoulders, behind his ears. His eyes move in an arc. Almost too thin, he has icy good looks —face sharp of features, sensual—the dark sensuality of barely contained violence.

The El Paso, Texas, sky is magic blue. Only the film of dusty gray which lingers on the horizon hints of the season of howling wind just passed, when the wind rampaged the city with racking regularity, the sun a dull whitish smear for days, dust settling only at night like filthy lace.

9

Now, a late summer, the sun spreads its warmth like an electric halo.

The grass on which they lie has lost its winter brittleness, assuming a velvet sheen. Here and there, trees on this truncated hill overlooking the rest of the park create alcoves, grottos. It's four o'clock. Shadows engraved by the bright stare of the sun provide pools for lovers.

But Cob and Shell lie in a clearing.

'You see him yet?' Shell demands impatiently.

'No—cool it.' Cob's legs curl about her more intimately.

'Maybe he fucking isn't here,' Shell says.

'I saw his fucking car,' Cob says.

'You're pressing too hard!' Shell repeats.

'Then why the fuck don't *you* get on top?' His dark eyes are intense periscopes.

In one quick motion, Shell mounts him. 'Like this?' A sudden bolting anger in her gesture, she arches her body over his, lunging downward fiercely from her hips.

He pushes her back roughly, his legs lock hers. Despite the proximity, a severe coldness seizes their bodies, fused together like pieces of ice.

Shell laughs coldly. 'How did it feel?' she fires at him.

'Shut up,' he admonishes. 'You'll fucking turn him off if he's already up here . . . Diggit! I think Manny spotted him, he's moving toward the fountain!'

'Raise my skirt higher,' Shell orders.

Cob raises it, revealing her tawny hips. Their lips crash on each other, cold like iron. Cob's hand strokes her breasts. Shell's body tenses. The amber eyes concentrate on the sky.

'He's seen us! He's hiding behind the bench!' Cob says victoriously.

Glancing back, Shell spots the man within a shadowed alcove. About fifty, wearing a business suit, he holds binoculars anxiously in his hands.

Behind him, in a tank shirt—his perennial uniform when he's not shirtless, to show off his well-muscled sixteen-year-old body—Manny, hair pushed determinedly over his forehead to create the impression of length, advances stealthily on the man.

Neck craning, the man watches Shell and Cob. The binoculars pressed against his eyes are like a terrible mask he's doomed to wear.

Cob pushes against Shell as if to penetrate her. She stares ferociously at him. His long black hair captures her face.

Pulled by the visual sensuality, the man abandons his crouching position. Perspiring, binoculars focused on the two, he whimpers in impotent frustration and secret joy. Rashly, he takes two steps toward them.

'He's moving nearer!' Cob whispers excitedly.

The cold movements of their bodies increase.

From behind, Manny pounces on the staring man.

Instantly their movements end; Shell and Cob rush toward the man and Manny. But already the panicked man is running down the hill to his car. The binoculars lie on the ground, an exposed secret.

Shell's eyes are fierce on Manny. 'You fucking let him get away!' she accuses.

'No, man,' Manny protests. 'You stopped too soon!'

'You fucking let him get away!' Cob badgers.

'No, man, *you* blew it,' Manny insists. 'You quit before I could even grab the weird fucker.'

Angrily Shell picks up the dropped binoculars. She studies them like the abandoned weapon of a stalked enemy. Depressed, she moves toward a stone bench under a wooden shelter on a loop of the park. A wall outlining it has begun to crumble, loose stones cascade down the spotted hill.

'Honest, Shell . . .' Manny approaches her. Not tall, Mexican-American—Chicano, he has the open good looks of a not very bright athlete. Yet, like Shell, like Cob, his face is branded by a bitter turn of the lips.

'Okay, man, fuck it,' Shell says impatiently. Just slightly past four! The afternoon stretches before them like a vast, barren desert.

'We could do something else.' Manny too feels the weight of the lingering afternoon.

'I wanted to get into *that* guy's head,' Shell says. 'Now he'll never come back.'

Cob lies lazily on the low stone wall.

Shell sees a boy sitting on a bench away from them. She focuses the binoculars on him. 'We need a fourth angel,' she says abruptly, removing the binoculars from her eyes as if something has affronted her gravely.

'Why?' Manny asks guiltily. An exposed board of the wooden shelter provides an excellent chinning bar. He begins to chin slowly.

Cob doesn't sit up. 'How about another chick?'

Despite the tone of indignation, as if she will not commit herself totally to that emotion, any emotion, a smile slashes Shell's face. 'Are you fucking calling *me* a chick, man?'

'You're not a fucking dude, are you?' Cob doesn't face her.

'I'm not a fucking *chick*, either,' she says. Part of her control, the cold smile remains. 'A chick is fucking weak and weird, diggit?'

'Okay.' Cob yawns. 'But if you want a fourth angel, why not a righteous chick?'

'I want a cat that won't fuck up.' Her words accuse them both. She glances at the boy on the bench.

'What do you say, Manny?' Cob asks him indifferently.

'Okay by me,' Manny says ambiguously, pleasing both.

'Now what the fuck does that mean?' Shell stands before him as he lowers himself.

'I mean, a dude, a chick—get a fucking dude, but don't get so fucking uptight,' Manny says. 'Why do you want a fourth angel?' He tries not to sound piqued.

'Because I'm fucking bored.' Shell stares at the boy on the bench as if to force him to look at her.

'So am I,' Cob accuses her back.

'Me, too,' Manny says sullenly. He removes his shirt, wipes his body with it. He flexes defiantly.

Cob laughs.

'What's so fucking funny?' Manny says.

'You are,' says Cob.

'Fuck you . . . Hey, check out that old woman, man!' Manny says.

A tangled puppet on high heels, a woman walks precariously toward them. A pitiful old hag, a brutal parody of youth, her face is screechingly painted in a vain attempt to mask deep, scar-deep, wrinkles. Her lips are a red quivering heart. Her dyed orange hair blazes unreally in the sun. Eyebrows arched like savage wings, her eyelashes are painted on her lids. Her dress is a crush of ruffles.

Cob touches his long hair, as if to assert the difference between her world and his.

Manny lets out a long whistle of mock approbation. 'We could get into *her* head,' he offers, anxious to make up for the earlier fiasco with the voyeur. 'I bet it's *loaded* with shit.'

'Leave her alone,' Shell says flatly. She turns quickly away from the woman. The boy on the bench has not even glanced at them.

'Why not her?' Manny asks.

'Yeah, why, Shell?' Cob challenges with seriousness. Occasionally, they hint of verbalizing the rivalry that developed from the moment they met, here, over a week ago; Manny came along a few days later.

Shell pulls their attention from the old woman. Abruptly: 'That cat over there—he could be the fourth angel.'

Still unaware of them, the youngman, their age, sits moodily on the back of a stone bench. He looks fixedly into his hands, holding sunglasses.

Cob reaches for the binoculars, fixes his sight through them on the boy.

'Shit, I think he's crying!'

'You're just saying that to bum Shell out on him cause she don't dig crying,' Manny laughs, amused to stir the shapeless conflict between Shell and Cob.

'No, man, I think the dude's fucking crying,' Cob says.

As if to intensify her naked focus on the boy, Shell's eyes narrow. 'We'll teach him how to stop,' she says sombrely.

Quickly, Shell leading, they approach the boy on the bench.

Very handsome, with longish brown hair, the boy covers his eyes quickly with the sunglasses. With a shake of his head he tosses his hair defiantly from his forehead.

'Are you crying?' The smile on Shell's face freezes as if before an enemy.

'No,' the boy says.

'Show us your eyes,' Cob says.

'Go to hell,' the boy tells them.

'Say, you're the dude whose mom died.' Manny recognizes him.

'Yeah . . . my mom . . .' The boy pauses. He can't pronounce the word 'died'. 'A month ago,' he says. A portion of his life rushed after her into death. A scream ripped from his throat, he ran insanely along the hospital corridor to dash himself against the windows as if within the windy darkness outside he would find her. Death a constant presence every moment of his existence now, she dies for him each brutal day.

His voice veers on anger. 'Look, I was just sitting here. Alone. I mean, what the hell . . . ?'

'What are you so uptight about?' Cob asks. Then, in a subdued tone: 'I lost my old lady too.'

'The fuck you did!' Shell turns on him.

A smile knives Cob's face. 'In a way,' he says. The smile flees. 'To my . . . sister.' Quickly he adjusts the purple glasses as if to block a tide of reality.

'What's your name?' Shell asks the boy.

'Jerry.'

'Manny's the one with the muscles, Cob's the thin one,' she introduces. 'And I'm Shell.'

'Shell?' Jerry is intrigued by her severe beauty.

'Like short for Michelle . . . Michelle, ma belle,' Manny sings the Beatles' song.

14

'It's not short for anything,' Shell says defiantly. 'Just Shell—like hard,' she seems to announce a credo.

Cob smiles.

'You want to be the fourth angel?' Shell asks Jerry abruptly.

'If being an angel means you're dead . . .' Jerry starts. 'What the hell is the fourth angel?' he shifts his thoughts.

'I'm the first angel, Cob's the second . . .' Shell says.

'No, man,' Cob corrects. '*I'm* the first angel, you're the second, Shell.'

Shell says: 'We'll find out.' Then to Jerry: 'So?'

'You mean like the Hell's Angels?' Jerry smiles.

'The Hell's Angels! Far fucking out!' Manny folds over with glee. He mimes the revving of a motorcycle. 'Varrooooo-mmmmmmmm!'

'We're like *Heaven's* Angels,' Shell says to Jerry.

'We just call ourselves angels, that's all,' Cob shrugs.

'What do I have to do?' Jerry asks, not taking them entirely seriously. Though he has always made friends easily, he has retained deliberately drawn boundaries between himself and others, as if the sea of emotion containing him and his mother may not be invaded. Since her death, he has isolated himself progressively, with memories.

Manny's hands form a halo over Jerry's head. '*Now* you're the fourth angel,' he says.

They all laugh.

Cob sees Jerry looking steadily at Shell. As if to scare the new boy, or test him: 'Have you ever done dope? You'll have to, with us,' he says.

Quickly fascinated, 'What kind of dope?' Jerry asks. A door may open to lead him from the void of death.

'Everything!' Manny says approvingly. 'Shell buys it! Diggit, her old man gives her *so* much bread, man! He digs her *so* much . . .'

The purple shield of Cob's eyes is still reflected on Jerry.

Jerry matches the steely stare, removes his own sunglasses.

Quickly Cob shifts his gaze, across the street, down the hill.

Shell's eyes follow his. To:

Three cars parked before the men's restroom. A fourth car just drove up.

'Another of those weird creeps rushing into the head,' Cob says with contempt.

'We could trap one and get into his head.' Shell studies Cob.

'Outasite,' Manny approves.

Cob nods solemnly. He looks like a young—sinister— prophet. A dark angel. Now he holds the abandoned binoculars to his eyes, over the purple glasses, looking at the men across the street. Like a sniper.

Jerry feels vaguely apprehensive.

'That's what the three angels—the *four* angels—do, man,' Manny explains to Jerry. 'We get into people's heads. We almost had a peeping Tom.'

His purple gaze suddenly again on Jerry, 'We interrogate people,' Cob says.

'About what?' Jerry asks.

'About all the bad shit,' Cob answers.

Now Shell is staring at the men cruising the restroom. One mills outside. She turns abruptly, studying Jerry's reaction. 'We could set fire to one of those guys down there,' she says.

2

'You're putting me on,' Jerry says quickly.

'Keep telling yourself that,' Cob tells him. 'Remember, you're the fourth angel now, you've got to go along with us.'

'Right on,' Manny says.

'You're still putting me on,' Jerry says defiantly.

Shell's gaze releases Jerry. 'Sure we're putting you on,' she says. 'Because that's not the kind of fire we dig. Inside, though,' she says, touching her chest, 'that's where we want to get—to set fires *inside*.' Now she touches her head, as if she can't determine where the origin of what she must discover is. 'Where the real heavy shit is.'

'What for?' Jerry asks.

'What for, Cob?' Shell shifts to him.

'To pass the fucking time,' Cob says lazily.

'What for, Manny?' Shell demands.

'Uh, cause . . . Whatever you say,' Manny shrugs.

Now Shell turns to Jerry: 'We do experience trips.'

'Just getting up each day . . .' Jerry starts.

Shell rushes words: 'Experience—so we can fucking cope with all the bad shit they're going to fucking throw at us, man—that's fucking why!' Anger in her voice: 'To survive you've got to learn not to feel, even if you have to *teach* yourself how.'

Their desperate excitement is catching. Jerry feels on probation. His mother's death plunged him into a profound emptiness, a howling desolation, which they may fill by helping him move relentlessly through the day, away from the knowledge of constant loss.

As if Shell's words had unlocked the troubled memories,

Manny blurts: 'Like me, man. Diggit, my old lady fucking had me picked up—at home, man, by the pigs; I was home—and she called the pigs and said I was a fucking runaway, pick me up.'

'She *wanted* you to run away,' Cob says harshly to Manny.

'That time, I spent a fucking week in the fucking juvenile detention home,' Manny says. 'That was only the first time—and she kept getting me fucking busted for runaway—in my own fucking house!' He goes on breathlessly: 'And diggit, while I was there, that old shit who runs the place fucking kept telling me to confess!'

'Confess!' Shell grabs the word.

'To what?' Cob asks.

'Like the old shit kept asking me how many times I done dope,' Manny says.

'Could you remember?' Cob laughs.

'Man, diggit, I kept telling the shit I never done any,' Manny goes on. 'And like he keeps insisting how many times, so I say, "Would you believe once?" and he says, "You confessed!" and diggit, man, I say, "Hell, no, man, I didn't say I *did* dope—I just asked would you believe once?" Man, it freaked him out!'

'Where did they interrogate you?' Shell asks, an idea forming.

'In a fucking small room. Dark except for one light. On me,' Manny says bitterly. He turns to Jerry, to explain something very important: 'At first I used to cry . . .'

'But no more,' Shell says emphatically.

'No more,' Manny repeats equally emphatically.

The summer sun is lingering on the horizon reluctant to surrender. But shadows are converging like warring giants under the tangle of trees. The fact that it's Friday augments the sense of desolation. The afternoon, the week will end—and nothing has happened. The voyeur escaped. A space of time passed, they did not move with it.

Cob says abruptly: 'There goes another creep into the head!'

Before the restroom, a man stands desolately, idly.

'*We'll* interrogate him!' Shell announces. Swiftly a desperate game forms: 'One of you cats go down to the head; whoever tries to come on with you, you bring him up here . . .'

Cob is caught quickly in the proposed plan: 'Jerry can go,' he says, testing him.

'No,' Jerry protests.

'You wanna be the fucking fourth angel or not?' Cob asks.

Jerry doesn't answer. He will not commit himself to their game. Not yet. Perhaps not at all.

'You go, Cob,' Shell says coldly.

An assault, readied? Cob braces; 'Why don't you, Shell? We'll trap . . .' he spews the word like bitter poison '. . . a dike.'

Cold, mutual smiles indicate a draw.

'The dude down there split, man,' Manny announces. 'He looked up the hill and saw us and freaked and fucking split.'

'There's too many of us, it's too open,' Shell agrees. 'We'll do it tonight,' she ends the afternoon's search.

Cob reacts like a jealous general not included in an important decision. 'Maybe I don't want to split yet,' he says.

'Okay,' Shell shrugs. She begins to walk away.

Glancing back uncertainly at Cob, Manny follows her. For seconds, Jerry remains with Cob. But they look away from each other. Now Jerry walks after Shell. Manny is running down the hill, hooting like a television Indian.

Coming down the hill deliberately slowly, sauntering, Cob finally joins them before Shell's parked car—new, shiny, expensive.

'I told you her old man loves her,' Manny tells Jerry, who's looking at the car.

Shell frowns. Then: 'I just blackmail him, that's all.' She laughs. She opens the car door quickly.

They get into the car. Cob in front with her, Manny and Jerry in the back, Shell drives out of the park with the expert skill of a racer. 'Where do you live?' she asks Jerry.

'I'm staying at my sister's,' Jerry says quickly. 'She lives alone, she's divorced.' Then: 'But I've got to stop at . . . my house first.' Where he lived with his mother. His mind sees her closed, vacant room, locked since her death.

'What for?' Cob seizes.

'To feed our cats,' Jerry says dully. Three cats. His and his mother's. He had tried taking them with him to his sister's, but the cats' panic had infected him. He returned them to the empty house; he goes there twice a day to feed them. And to be with memories of her. 'We'll be selling the house soon . . .' Another end, another loss, another death. Quickly, he gives Shell directions.

They're there: before an old stately, two-storey house with white columns. Already it has the look of a house sorrowfully abandoned. The grass, uncut, has been invaded by flowery weeds.

'I dig old pads,' Cob says, 'let's see the inside.' He's opening the car door.

'No!' Jerry's abrupt protest surprises him. 'It'll just take a minute to feed the cats.' He realized: he doesn't want them in that house. Why? He's already out of the car.

Inside the graceful old house: enormous rooms, chandeliers, carpets—bespeaking a wealth which faded many years ago with his father's death—an incident that is the barest ghost of a memory from his early childhood.

Instantly the cavernous sighing loneliness of the house suffuses him.

Two long-haired cats approach him soundlessly. But the third, his mother's favorite, a mysterious cat, a beautiful, sleek Burmese female with hair like brown velvet, moves away from him. Feeling the emptiness. Not understanding, does she blame him? He strokes the two furry ones, hoping the third will join them.

But she remains away, as she has from him and the other cats since death overwhelmed their world; remains staring at him with yellow eyes. Then she moves up the stairs. Jerry follows her slowly. The cat waits before the locked door. Quickly Jerry turns away from his mother's room: vacant, empty. Empty.

Outside in Shell's car: 'He didn't fucking want us in his house!' Cob says indignantly.

'I know,' Shell says.

Jerry is back. 'Okay,' he says. The yellow eyes of the brown Burmese feline haunt him.

Shell is driving in a direction opposite to the one Jerry gave her as his sister's. Matching their cool, he doesn't question where they're going. There's the suddenly welcome promise of discovery, of crammed experience.

Speeding along a wide street, past rushing desert hills.

Resenting that Shell has not told him where they're going—and he suspects she has no definite plan—rashly Cob grabs for control of the shapeless situation: 'We're going to an old house near the freeway.'

'No, man,' Shell says firmly, like a slap at him. 'Not there.'

Anger, bewilderment. Cob doesn't glance at her. She had understood, and she had challenged him.

'But later we'll go there,' Shell says after moments of victorious silence.

As if his mind had chosen to open compulsively, incongruously, at this moment, Manny blurts crazily: 'We all love each other!'

Shell parks abruptly. Before them looms a large Catholic church. Its crosses are thrust angrily like spears at heaven.

Jerry looks bitterly at the church. Whatever death is, that church represents the black mystery which seized his mother. And he hates it.

They get out of the car.

'We're going in there?' Manny says, aghast. Automatically he begins to make the sign of the cross, stops, embarrassed. Instead, he puts on his shirt.

'Where else would you fucking become a fourth angel?' Cob seizes leadership from Shell and warns Jerry ambiguously.

On the steps leading into the church, Shell coolly removes a small cellophane packet from the inside of her blouse.

'You gonna light that shit here?' Manny asks admiringly.

'Why the hell not?' Cob obviates the rashness of Shell's gesture. 'Stoned is the only way to do a church.'

Feeling tested, Jerry remains quiet. A spark of apprehension melds into excitement and anticipation.

Shell rolls a joint of grass, she moistens the paper with her tongue. Openly, as if it were an ordinary cigarette, she lights it. She inhales deeply, passes it to Cob; he inhales even more deeply. Then it's Manny's turn. Now Jerry's. They watch him carefully —they know it's his first time. A double challenge, to do the dope and to do it openly, before the church.

Imitating them, Jerry inhales deeply, deeply, holds the smoke. He waits eagerly for a magical reaction to the vaunted weed.

The joint nothing but a roach now, Shell improvises a holder by splitting a match into two slivers, creating a pincer. When they can no longer hold the roach even with the pincer, on the edge of a match Shell fires what remains of the weed, blows it out, and holds it for Cob, then Manny, then Jerry to sniff the smoke.

'I don't feel anything,' Jerry says impatiently. What he does feel—starkly—is the presence of the church. The sun shatters on a mosaicked window depicting a great-winged angel slaying a dragon. The stained glass bleeds luminous colors.

They light another number, passing it around like tribal Indians. Cars along the street drive by obliviously.

Shell's look questions Jerry.

'Nothing,' he says flatly, the one word an accusation of the weed and them. He desperately wants the euphoria, even momentary, that is making Manny giggle uncontrollably.

'You're probably on downers,' Cob judges Jerry back.

Jerry doesn't answer. But is that the reason? The tranquilizers—sleeping pills, and they had been his mother's—he's taken daily since her death?

'We'll get you stoned,' Shell says.

'Right,' Cob agrees coldly.

'What if the priest sees us turning on here?' Manny questions suddenly.

'We'll turn *him* on,' Cob tosses.

Shell pulls open the heavy wooden door into the church. Inside, gaudily painted statues of saints ignore them, stare instead as if at a stone heaven. Candles in wine-colored glasses glisten like electric teardrops. At the feet of the crucified Jesus over the awesome altar, the sun melts the windows' colors like dyed wax blood on the floor.

Except for themselves—and the statues like stark dead presences—the church is empty.

Concealing his movements from the others, Manny half-kneels. Surreptitiously, he dips his fingers into the bowl of holy water—but does not touch his forehead with it.

Jerry stares ferociously at the altar. He feels sorrow for the crucified figures, yes—and defiance toward the savage God that murdered his mother.

Cob looks with curiosity about the church. 'Far, *far* out,' he approves.

Shell opens the door of the confessional booth. With mock solemnity, she sits inside it.

'For Chrissakes, Shell, what the hell are you into?' Manny is openly horrified now. 'It's the house of God,' he blurts memorized words.

'The house of God, huh?' Cob says. 'Then *He* must dig tripping—He sure digs far-out colors.'

'I'm going to play priest,' Shell whispers back at Manny. 'And you're all going to confess.'

Manny giggles nervously. Seriously: 'You can't hear confessions, man, you're not like ordained.'

Cob joins Shell's game: 'You don't dig, Manny, it's not the priest you confess to, it's the booth; like the *booth* is wired to God.'

'Shit, man,' Manny laughs. Then fearfully he looks at the altar.

Jerry has not moved. He wants God to see him, to know of his defiance. He wants to yell it out.

In a parody of confessor, stunningly beautiful, a splash of

23

color in the gray darkness of the confessional booth, Shell crosses her hands on her lap. 'Who the hell is going to be first?' she whispers.

Manny is laughing hysterically now.

'You, Manny!' Cob asserts himself.

'Man, I tole you,' Manny says. 'I already like confessed to the old shit at the J.D. home, man, like I *tole* you.'

'This time it's different.' Shell's strange game shapes. 'This time you can confess for other people—how *they've* shit on you. Like confess for the old dude that fucked you over in the home.'

'Far out!' Doubled over with glee, Manny enters one side of the confessional booth. He half-kneels. Through the small screened window he faces Shell.

'Confess *their* sins,' Shell tries to imitate the voice of a gruff priest.

Between nervous giggles, Manny whispers in mock confession: 'Father . . . I mean, Sister-Priest, I'm the old shit from the J.D. home. Like I run it, dig, and I want to confess that I dig beating up on all the bad-ass kids.'

Joining them suddenly—a manifestation of his defiant rebellion—Jerry explains to Shell: 'Now you're supposed to ask How Many Times. They always ask How Many Times. Like that's how they give penance.'

'I'd dig giving penance,' Cob says softly.

Shell intones: 'How many fucking times?'

Manny says: 'As many times as it takes to give them an ass they can't sit on.' He bursts into loud laughter. He continues: 'Dig, Priest-Lady? There's this one bad-ass dude, man. His name is Manny and his mother calls the pigs to have him busted as incorrigible and runaway . . .'

'Confess for *her*—for your old lady!' Cob exhorts excitedly. He leans against the booth, listening intently.

'Yes!' Shell's approval comes like the lashing of an angry whip.

Now Manny speaks in the falsetto of a woman: 'Dear Lady-

24

Priest, I want to confess to how I have fucked over my bad-ass son.'

Quickly Jerry moves away from this part of the game. He turns to the sun-illumined window, to the savage angel and the flailing dragon of evil bleeding at his feet.

'And diggit, Priest-Lady,' Manny is going on, 'I don't have no husband, but I have . . .' The laughter wanes. 'See, when I call the pigs to take my Manny away, like they just come in and . . .' the voice becomes his own . . . 'and they put the fucking handcuffs on me and take me and I'm fingerprinted, man, and they take my fucking clothes away, and then that shit tries to get a confession outa *my* head, instead of hers, my old lady's —and all she says to me when she goes to see me there is she's sorry, she's sorry.' Manny tries to force laughter.

'How many times?' Shell says.

'Shit, man, she sent me to that J.D. home at least a half-dozen times. Every time she . . . every time . . .' He stops abruptly.

'Every time she what? You've *got* to say!' Shell demands.

'Otherwise you can't give penance,' Cob says.

Manny lowers his head. 'Every time she's fucking got a new boyfriend.'

A glance of a frown touches Cob's face.

'How many times?' Shell continues relentlessly.

'Over and over!' Manny gasps.

'*How many goddam times, Manny?*' Shell demands fiercely now. 'How many boyfriends!'

'I fucking stopped counting!' Manny almost-yells.

'Estimate!' Shell commands.

'As many times as she's sent me away. More!' Manny says. 'But this last time, she had a change of fucking heart . . .'

'A change of what?' comes Shell's cold voice.

'Heart! Heart!' Manny flings the word.

'That's what pumps the blood in the body,' Cob says.

'And it only changes when you die,' Shell finishes.

'See,' Manny's words are tortured now, 'she wants me to call her new boyfriends father! And I said fuck you, and she calls the pigs, and this time the old shit sends me to Gatesville, the prison for boys; they shackled our ankles with chains, we didn't even know where they were taking us, we didn't have no fucking trial—nothing! . . . Then I ran away from there!'

'Ran away? Where?' Cob is puzzled.

Manny laughs bitterly. Then he whispers, almost inaudibly, in a small voice, 'Home. Back to her . . .'

Shell's lips fire words at him: 'Don't fucking cry, Manny!'

'Who's fucking crying!' Manny protests. 'I don't ever fucking cry!'

Suddenly Jerry accosts Shell: 'Stop it!'

'Why?' Cob demands.

'Because he's upset—really upset,' Jerry says.

Shell's voice emerges frozen from the booth: 'You don't dig, Jerry. Like we're helping him—we're helping him to stop *feeling*, so he'll never even *want* to cry.'

To stop feeling . . . Jerry thinks.

'Besides, Manny's just faking being all uptight,' Cob says.

'Yeah, yeah,' Manny says anxiously, 'like I'm not uptight at all.'

'Now penance,' Cob reminds eagerly.

'Yeah, I got to lay some heavy penance on them,' Manny says, his voice controlled.

'Give them hell,' Shell says. She's still looking at Jerry.

'What does the old shit who runs the J.D. home get, man?' Cob coaxes.

'He gets . . . The penance is . . . The sentence will be . . .' Manny begins. 'He'll have to . . . He'll fucking have to . . .' He closes his eyes, concentrating, his hands pressed against his forehead as if to squeeze out an enormous judgment. '*She'll* have to . . . My mother will have to . . . !' But he can't finish. Quickly he leaves the booth.

A long, long silence. The golden angel, the slain dragon, the eyeless statues—and the crucified figure—command the hollow church.

'Now you, Cob,' Shell says.

'That's your trip,' Cob answers quickly.

'Wouldn't you like to pass penance on your old man for leaving you?' Shell pursues relentlessly. 'Or on your old lady?'

Cob blanches, but his lips smile.

'Or on your sister,' Shell pronounces.

'She's not . . .' Cob begins. 'And you, Shell?' he thrusts back swiftly.

'On my . . .' She stops, too. 'But it's Jerry's initiation, he's the fourth angel.'

The sun has fled the mosaicked window. Both the dragon and the saint seem vanquished.

'Let's split,' Manny says, as if coming out of a daze.

'Not until the fourth angel tells us who he'd sentence,' Shell says from the booth.

'Who, man?' Cob insists.

Jerry looks at the altar. Then he says, 'I'd sentence God.'

3

'Now what?'

Manny asked that question as if expecting a verdict. A hollow of time exists as they stand outside the church, the stained-glass window muted in the late Texas afternoon. Clouds like gauze are pasted on the orange horizon.

'We could go to Jerry's pad,' Cob insists.

Jerry doesn't answer. He knows: He doesn't want them to invade memories of his mother in that house. He feels a marked tension between him and Cob. Over his persistence that they go to his house? Or also over Shell? Has she made it with him?—with Manny? the thought flashes, important.

'No—we'll go to the old house by the freeway,' Shell releases Jerry quickly.

'You have a house to yourselves?' Jerry asks.

'Yeah—angel headquarters,' Manny says. 'Cob discovered it.'

'A boarded-up house,' Shell tells him. 'They're going to knock it down. Until they do, it's ours.'

An erratic breeze captures a frantic sheet of paper. Abandoned, the paper glides, then falls lightly on the street like a dead bird.

'And there's a weird bar at the corner,' Cob says.

'My sister's waiting for me for dinner,' Jerry says hurriedly. An excuse to get away from them? Suddenly, to withdraw. No, not a withdrawal—a postponement. He wants to be with them again.

'We all have to split,' Shell says. 'I've got to say goodbye to my old lady, she's going to the fucking beauty farm.'

'Again?' Cob asks derisively.

'Yeah, again,' Shell says flatly.

'She pays like a thousand dollars a day at that beauty farm,' Manny exaggerates, impressed by Shell's wealth. Then abruptly, feeling alone: '*I* don't have to split yet.'

'Your mother's with some new dude?' Cob aims.

'Who's *yours* with?' Manny snaps.

'His sister,' Shell says.

Cob turns abruptly toward her.

But Shell ends the hostile interlude: 'I'll pick you up after dinner,' she tells them. 'We'll do the interrogation then.'

'Far out!' Manny agrees.

'Who are you going to interrogate?' Jerry asks softly.

'*We*, man; who are *we* going to interrogate,' Shell corrects. 'You're the fourth angel.'

'Maybe we'll interrogate you,' Cob tosses at Jerry.

'We don't interrogate each other,' Shell deserts Cob.

'No?' Cob smiles. Quickly: 'I'll drive this time, man,' he says to Shell.

Shell shrugs coolly. But instead of getting in front with him, she sits in the back of the car with Jerry.

His proximity to her—a warmth touches Jerry's body. Despite his desire to withdraw for now, he's glad they'll be together later, even if he'll withhold his commitment to their experience, whatever it will be. There's the howling void of loss. To fill it with their motion!

They left Jerry at his sister's. He stares after them as the car dashes away—Cob clearly trying to outdrive Shell. Jerry feels a new part of his life may be beginning, with them, another part may be dying. But does he want it to die? It belongs to his mother.

After dinner. He waits anxiously for them outside.

There they are. Shell is driving, Cob is in front with her. They haven't picked Manny up yet.

But he's waiting for them before a broken-down house. An old couch—gutted, cotton bowels spilling—squats heavily on a rickety porch. 'I don't know how late!' Manny calls back in

Spanish to someone inside the dilapidated house. He gets in the car. 'My old lady bums me out all the fucking time. She sends me off to that fucking J.D. home whenever she wants me out of the way, but she always wants to fucking know when I'll be home.'

They drive away.

Night is coming down, an arc of blue still lights the edge of the sky.

Shell parks the car in an alley behind a boarded-up house.

Its windows are blinded by nailed crossed boards—stark X's like marks signaling imminent destruction. Grassless, its lawn is covered by accumulated weeds. The house seems to be waiting desolately for the hungry machines that will devour it and spill it out as dust. Tangled grotesquely as if they had clawed each other to death in a desperate battle, tumbleweeds crouch against the walls. Wounded. Dead.

On the corner of the same block is a bar—obviously popular from the many cars already parked in the surrounding lot. As if to shut out curious eyes, its windows are painted black.

The four get out of the car. Shell is carrying a paper-towel tube, the towels gone, and a large flashlight, unlit. Wearing the purple glasses even in the twilit dark, Cob carries a transistor radio, turned up now on the savagely beautiful sounds of the Rolling Stones.

From a back window, they draw loose boards apart, and they climb into the abandoned house; they replace the boards carefully in dooming X's.

Inside: large, empty, echoing rooms drowning in the odor of enclosed emptiness, trapped space. Light from the cars speeding along the ramp to the freeway rushes rashly through gapes in the crossed boards and into the house, revealing, in flashes, walls peeling in monster shapes.

'This is angel headquarters,' Manny laughs. His words echo eerily.

They've entered what was obviously the living-room. There's a gutted, crumbling fireplace, powdered cement like ashes on the floor. Electrical wires have been cut; like severed veins. The house is dead. Jerry feels as if he's moved physically into the empty part of himself.

Shell sits on the decaying floor. Immediately she begins to work mysteriously on the towel tube. Manny sits down too. Facing each other across the gray darkness, Jerry and Cob remain standing. Then Cob breaks the tense closeness by sitting down. An outsider, stretching the time of his deliberate exile, Jerry remains standing for long moments. Finally he joins them on the floor. He sits between Shell and Cob.

Carefully, Shell has cut a round hole the size of a fifty-cent piece into the cardboard funnel. Now she's covering the hole with a strip of tinfoil, which she secures with masking tape. She depresses the portion over the hole. With a pin brooch, a golden subdued eye in the darkness, she punches several holes into the tinfoil. From a plastic bag she's removed from the pocket of her skirt, she takes out a brownish-green chunk and fills the hollow. Now she smiles at Jerry: 'This'll stone you.'

'It's hash,' Manny announces.

'It'll get you so righteous ripped,' Cob promises Jerry.

Jerry feels excited. Escape!

Legs crossed, they move closer together in a rectangle. Shell presses the improvised pipe to her mouth. Cob holds a match to the hash as her palm alternately covers and uncovers the open end.

Retaining the smoke she drew, Shell leans over, holding the pipe to Cob's lips, still working her palm against the opening to allow the air in. He hits. Now she holds the pipe for Manny They are involved in a ritual, with rules. Now she includes Jerry in the ritual.

He inhales, feels the smoke in his lungs and almost coughs it out, holds it. Waits expectantly.

Then the mysteriously intimate ritual is played again. This time Cob holds the pipe to his own lips, then to theirs. They take turns holding the pipe, passing it from mouth to mouth until the hash is smoked.

Seized by the mellowing mood, Shell leans back on the floor, floating in the darkness. Manny lies down. Cob sighs. The music from the radio evaporates into the dark air.

Jerry concentrates. What does he feel? What do *they* feel? With bitter disappointment, he says aloud: 'I don't feel anything.'

Wordlessly, Shell fills another pipe with hash. She holds it to Jerry's mouth, Cob lights it. Jerry inhales deeply, deeply, withdraws.

'More,' Shell says.

Jerry inhales from it again.

'More!' Shell repeats.

Again Jerry hits.

'More!' Shell holds the pipe relentlessly to his mouth, hardly allowing him an interval to breathe. 'More!'

Jerry inhales audibly.

'Are you stoned now?' Shell demands.

Jerry waits before answering. He wants to join them. But nothing. He shakes his head.

'It's the downers,' Cob says.

'*I'm* stoned,' Manny giggles. 'Man, I am so fucking messed up and ripped! I got off on the first hit, man!'

Now: A silence. The silence of the house raided by the melting rock sounds from the radio.

What Jerry does feel is Shell's sensuality. He stares openly at her, so close—so calm suddenly.

'You dig her?'

At first Jerry didn't know who had spoken the easy words, they came without origin out of the darkness—as if pulled from his mind. It was Cob who spoke them.

In the cloudy darkness, Shell's expression is intact.

Manny giggles: 'Shell, man . . . Shell . . . She's really . . . Wow!'

'Do *you*?' Jerry asks Cob back.

Shell sits up. Her laughter rushes into the empty dark house.

Manny says: 'Shell don't dig anyone, right, Shell?'

'Right,' she says. Then: 'Just us! The four angels!'

She has allowed—forced—Jerry and Cob to withdraw.

Now minutes flow with the music, which mingles with the advancing darkness as night invades the old house, swallowing even the outlines of dim shadows.

'What about my interrogation?' Manny asks. Shooting out of his mind, mangled memories—the J.D. home! The interrogation: 'Confess! You do grass, acid, smack?' Solitary! The cramped filthy cell! His arm wrenched back, a fist blackening his vision! Cockroaches! Filth! And the sound of others shouting!

'Yeah, we've got to do Manny's interrogation,' Shell says.

'Who are we going to interrogate?' Jerry asks again. We ... But will he flow with them in the current they choose? Will he stay?

'A faggot from that queer bar at the corner,' Cob clarifies viciously.

The drug's mellowness has ended abruptly.

Suddenly the four are standing.

'We need a decoy,' Shell says.

'Jerry,' Cob chooses.

An aspect of unreality springing darkly into reality. Stirrings of a new anger. But: 'I wouldn't know what to do,' Jerry withdraws from the sparking excitement.

A sinister, dark-glassed presence in the black room, 'We'll tell you,' Cob says.

'Why not you, Cob?' Jerry tosses.

'Yeah, Cob, how about you?' Shell asks.

'Because I've got to be here,' Cob says.

'Why?' Shell challenges.

Cob answers himself: Because otherwise you'll be in control. Aloud he says: 'Jerry's the new angel.'

'Man, if the dude don't want to . . .' Manny starts.

'Do you want to, Manny?' Shell asks him. Is there a hint of accusation?

'It's not that I *want* to, it's just that if like the dude don't *want* to . . .' Manny feels slightly on trial.

'Okay. Manny,' Shell chooses, releasing Jerry.

I'll never see my mother again, the thought *almost* forms on Jerry's mind as if he's about to surrender one world to another.

4

Jerry's world: A voice has been stilled, a body has disappeared. And his need of his mother is unchanged. That is death: sudden silence. And frozen memories. The despised hospital. And the next night—or the next?—time was a black ocean surrounding him—when was it that he sat outside the locked mortuary where her body lay?—sat under the dark sky and kept a silent vigil.

Quickly now, he looks at Shell, Cob, Manny. They stand outside in the waiting night. To stir time, 'Let's start!' Jerry hears his enraged words.

'Like the cat's really up for it now,' Cob says. Satisfaction? Resentment?

'The interrogation!' Manny says eagerly.

Stars are clear in the field of sky.

From cars parked in the lot surrounding the crowded bar, young and youngish men and women move into it, occasionally stopping to talk to someone recognized.

The large flashlight in her hand like a weapon, Shell studies the milling groups. 'Okay,' she assumes command. 'We'll stay here, and you'll go out to the lot, Manny. When you have someone, we'll split inside and wait for you.'

'What'll I do?' Manny asks cautiously.

'Just hang around the lot,' Cob says.

'And look like you're really up for making it,' Shell instructs. Resistance to commit himself to this adventure. For a few

35

moments Jerry wants to leave. But the empty night contains death. He'll commit himself in stages.

An ambiguous smile wounds Cob's wolfish face: he retains his dark-purple stare steadily on Jerry.

Carried by the excitement of the approaching adventure, Manny has moved quickly into the car lot.

'Why do you keep looking up?'

Shell's words surprised Jerry; he realizes he's looking at the sky, clear but black like on the night of his lonesome vigil outside the mortuary.

'Just looking at the sky,' he attempts to dismiss. But the memory of death choked his voice.

Shell's words assault with unexpected brutality: 'And the sky makes you want to cry?'

'I'm just looking at the sky,' Jerry says angrily. Now his words come in bewilderment: 'The sky seems so dark since my Mom . . .' Unexpectedly he blurts: 'I locked the room immediately after!'

'What room?' Shell seizes.

'Her bedroom. I locked it. I haven't opened it since.' Jerry's voice almost breaks again.

Cob glances quickly at Shell.

She looks back at him as if exchanging a silent message.

Then, in a controlled voice, so controlled that her words are almost whispered, Shell says to Jerry: 'Diggit: crying is the worst shit. When you cry, it's all over for you because that's when the shit takes over. When you cry, you're through.'

'We'll teach you to stop,' Cob's tone matches Shell's as he echoes her words of this afternoon.

'You don't have to teach me anything!' Jerry says firmly. 'I wasn't crying.' And he has conquered the welling tears.

'Good,' Shell smiles.

A tension, a closeness. The three stand in the shadows of the alley, watching Manny.

Flexing, his hands in his pockets to tense his muscles, Manny

36

leans against a car in the lot. Three youngmen on their way to the bar pause to look at him.

Quickly, one of the group—he could have been twenty, thirty—makes an about-face toward Manny.

In the alley: 'Watch him fuck up,' Cob predicts.

'No,' Jerry defends Manny, 'he'll be okay.' The boundary of his commitment is extending.

In the car lot: 'Hi!' The youngish-man's eyes reveal his age as closer to thirty.

'Hi,' Manny answers. He doesn't know what to do.

Silence.

'Are you hustling?' the youngish man blurts.

Echoes of talk in the detention home; the state institution. Youngmen bragging about hustling other men. Manny understands. But he doesn't answer, he doesn't know what this man wants to hear. 'Well—uh . . .' he stutters.

The youngish man sighs. 'You are,' he determines sadly. 'And I don't go for that. Good luck.' He walks away.

In the alley: 'He fucked up!' Cob blurts.

'Give him a chance,' Jerry says.

'*You* want to go?' Shell shoots at Cob.

In the parking lot: Manny turns frantically toward the shadowed alley. Are the three judging him? . . . Often it seems to him that he's on the brink of an unjustified verdict, an undeserved sentence.

Another group of youngmen on their way to the bar is approaching. They pass him without acknowledgment. Panic! Then: Interminable empty moments:

Broken suddenly by the presence of a very effeminate youngman clearly in his early twenties. 'Hello!' he approaches Manny aggressively. 'You want to come with me? I've got a nice place and lots of booze!'

'Booze!' Manny says indignantly.

The effeminate youngman says uncertainly: 'Don't you drink?'

'Oh, uh, yeah, sure, man,' Manny says carefully. 'But I got a better idea,' he rushes.

'Really?' the effeminate youngman says deliriously.

'That house over there,' Manny points to the boarded house. He can discern the outlines of the three in the murky shadows. 'It's empty. We could like go there, man.'

'Is it safe?' the effeminate youngman hesitates.

'Yeah, sure,' Manny is impatient, knowing Shell and the others are watching.

The youngman is becoming progressively more effeminate, like a very young but very aggressive girl. 'But my place is so much more private—I've got a car.'

'The house is closer,' Manny says.

The youngman cocks his head—and now he's the complete parody of a girl: 'You *are* horny . . . Okay, let's go!'

In the alley: 'He's hooked! Let's go inside!' Cob says.

But Shell makes no move. 'He's like a girl,' she says.

'So what?' Cob confronts Shell.

Approaching the dead house, Manny realizes with bewilderment that the three are still standing outside. What's wrong? Now Shell is actually coming toward them! What the hell!

'Who is *she*?' the effeminate youngman blurts.

'I'm his sister,' Shell says toughly. Cob and Jerry wait nearby. 'What the fuck are you doing with my brother?'

'Oh, Christ,' the effeminate youngman says despondently.

'You'd better fucking split!' Shell says to him.

The effeminate youngman sees Jerry and Cob now; he retreats quickly. Now he's running.

Jerry feels relief. The interrogation has been aborted.

'What the fuck is the matter with you, Shell?' Cob demands angrily. 'You deliberately blew it!'

'Yeah, man, what the fuck is this?' Manny asks.

'He was wrong, that's all,' Shell says quietly.

Cob studies her harshly. Then he laughs loudly, as if he's

glanced at an exposed secret. 'You know, Shell, you're really funny.'

'One day I'll fucking show you how funny I can fucking be,' Shell warns. But a smile clings determinedly to her face.

'You don't scare me, Shell.' Cob's dark-shielded eyes trap her.

'Why should I want to?' Shell asks him. Quickly to Manny: 'You'll have to go get another guy, man.'

Manny moves back to the car lot. He doesn't understand, but he wants to avoid a hassle.

The three retreat back into the shadows of the alley.

In the parking lot Manny waits. He should have insisted they interrogate that guy. He smiles, imagines a confrontation with Shell.

'You always smile?'

Manny sees a man in his upper twenties, tall, well-dressed; slender, good-looking, masculine; his hair is longish, his sideburns are full.

'Oh, uh, yeah, I smile a lot,' Manny chooses his words carefully.

In the alley: Stirring shadows: Jerry, Cob, Shell.

'He'll do!' Shell says.

'Maybe he won't come, though,' Jerry says, and hopes suddenly the man won't, that the scene will end now. And with Shell's anger. Yes, Shell's anger in defeat. He faces his antagonism toward her too, antagonism mixed with desire. Deliberately he moves out of the heavy darkness, his outline thrust into the wing of the corner streetlight.

'You want the dude to see you?' Cob's words are both question and accusation.

Jerry doesn't move.

In the parking lot:

'How old are you?' the man asks Manny.

'Eighteen,' Manny lies.

The man smiles warmly. 'Usually, with very young people I don't . . . You have a fantastic body,' he tells Manny, as if a conflict is occurring within him. 'What's your name?' he's suddenly embarrassed.

'Manny.'

'Mine's Stuart—they call me Stu,' he says quickly.

'Hi, Stu,' Manny says.

'Would you like to come with me?' the man rushes words. 'I'm staying at a motel, and tomorrow, Saturday, we could go swimming. Would you like to come with me?' His voice is urgent, as if he must struggle to form each word.

'I got a better idea,' Manny says.

The man's body relaxes at the implied agreement. 'What idea?' he asks. But he doesn't really care; he's ferociously excited by Manny, the materialization of the sex fantasies of so many times.

'That old house over there,' Manny points. 'It's empty, man, and like we could go there.'

Glancing at the gauzy gray outline of the house, the man feels an instant of intruding fear. 'But the motel would be more comfortable,' he says.

'Well, see, the only thing is,' Manny hears his own words in shock, 'see, I gotta get home early before my old lady calls the pigs to pick me up again.'

'You're married?' Stuart asks incredulously.

'No, no, man,' Manny says with impatience. 'My old lady— my mother . . .' Rage clutches him: His mother! The cops! The interrogation at the detention home! The angry light under which he was questioned, beaten! And for what reason?

'You mean you're hiding in that house? You ran away?' Curiously, Stuart is even more excited now. Desire smothers fear.

'Kind of, uh . . .' Manny doesn't know what to say. Will the man be frightened now? Manny adds: 'Tomorrow, man—like I could meet you tomorrow, and *then* we'd do the motel.'

Stuart smiles. Then fear recurs on the surface of desire. Quickly it drowns in longing. 'Okay,' he agrees, 'the house over there—and the motel tomorrow.'

40

'Outasite,' Manny says.

In the alley: Shell, Cob, and Jerry climb swiftly through the window, into the empty house. They move through it, along the hall. Into the living-room: darker now. In the darkness, the three wait quietly pressed against the walls.

Outside: Excited, happy, Stuart follows Manny. 'I bet a lot goes on inside that house,' he says.

'Yeah, Stu,' Manny says, and laughs.

Through the window, they enter the dark house. 'I can't see a thing,' Stuart says. Now his burgeoning desire has conquered all fear.

'Follow me,' Manny says.

Stuart follows Manny's dark shadow along the corridor. 'Where are we?' he laughs.

In the living-room Manny leads Stuart tensely to the middle of it.

Suddenly a savage white light crashes on the man's face.

Swiftly abandoning him in the pool of light, Manny flees against the wall.

The blazing white light shatters on Stuart. Off! On! Off! On! He blinks in terror. 'Manny?' he calls. His body is seized by icy fear. 'Manny!' he calls urgently. 'Who's holding that light?' he demands.

Shell continues to aim the flashlight on him. Off! On!— each burst of frozen light like a bullet.

Suddenly Stuart bolts toward the door. Out of the darkness, Cob's hands grab him roughly, push him violently back into the center of the room. Shell's light captures him fiercely again in its glaring, now steady, white eye.

Disgust knives Jerry.

'Manny, what is this?' the man yells.

'The interrogation!' come Manny's cold words from the dark. 'Like they did to me.'

Trembling, the man slides against the wall. Jerry sees the desperate shadow. Remembers himself dashing in panic along the hospital corridor, from—to—death. Impulsively he reaches

41

out to hold the man firmly by the shoulders, to contain the man's panic, to calm him.

But frightened by the reaching hands, Stuart breaks away with an anguished gasp.

'Cool it, cool it,' Jerry says urgently. 'You'll be okay; just cool it!'

Aware of Jerry's threatening vacillation and to create the momentum that will erode it, 'What's your name!' Shell demands of Stuart, her voice tears the darkness like lightning.

'Stuart!' the man reacts. 'They call me Stu . . .' The words are automatic; their familiarity attempts to order this jagged unreality.

Swiftly Shell turns the light on Manny.

Through light-assaulted vision, Stuart sees Manny—and he thinks crazily: He'll help me!

'That's Manny,' Shell's voice announces, 'you've already met.' Then quickly she moves the light on Cob. 'And that's Cob.'

Stuart faces the sinister purple gaze. The sunglasses reflect the light in two brutal accusing thrusts.

Shell shifts the light abruptly to Jerry. 'That's Jerry.' She holds it on him steadily. Long. Very long. Longer. Much longer than on the others: as if finally he too may be interrogated?

Jerry blinks. The light traps him in the man's panic. Yet excitement bolts: melding with disgust, gnawing into it, conquering it.

'And she's Shell!' Cob calls from the darkness. 'Show him!' his voice orders.

Slowly Shell holds the light under her chin. Her illumined face is a deliberately distorted apparition. The beautiful features pulled grotesquely by shadows, she looks infinitely evil. 'I'm Shell.'

The light crashes back on Stuart.

'Manny, I trusted you!' the man founders.

'And I trusted you too,' Manny's voice breaks as if it isn't Stuart he's speaking to.

'But I didn't do anything to you,' Stuart tries to reason.

'Neither did I,' Manny's strange voice says. Manny's world:
In a vague trance. Another place, another time, other people.

Shell's voice inundates the darkness: 'Which one do you
want, Stu?'

The man knows the night's terror is only beginning.

5

Suddenly Shell turned off the flashlight. Darkness caves in on the room. There's the sound of footsteps shifting, moving in about the man. Now: petrified silence. Stuart stands perfectly still—from where will the assault spring?

Jerry's mind is cluttered. Waves of new excitement roar. At the same time, he wants to flee the terrible scene. Try to help the man? Prove himself strong in this violent initiation? Smash at life? Destroy his own vulnerability?

'You haven't answered, Stu. Which one do you want?' Shell's voice is even. At her side the flashlight is a dormant weapon.

'I don't know what you mean,' Stuart says quietly.

'The fuck you don't!' Cob assaults. He fires brutally: 'Queer!'

'Now wait . . .' the man starts. 'You have no right!'

'*Queer!*' Cob repeats in ferocious judgment.

'You've got it wrong.' Stuart attempts to shift their intense scrutiny.

'Sure we fucking have,' Manny derides, reminding himself that this is *his* interrogation.

Shell sits on the floor, Manny follows, then Cob: a triangle enclosing the man. Purposely not following them, Jerry remains standing.

'What do you want from me?' Stuart remains still, as if any movement may stir the violence out of the dark.

'What *do* you want from him?' Jerry questions aloud. And his mind proceeds silently—and from me?

'We want to get into your head, man. Into every locked room,' Shell says.

To Stuart? To me? Jerry wonders. A threat? Every locked room . . . The uncommitted outsider, he still stands.

Now Stuart's voice comes with deliberate control: 'I'm leaving. If you try to stop me . . . There are people outside, they'll call the police.'

'You try it, and I'll . . .' Cob's voice strikes like an iron chain.

Shell says: 'Diggit, Stu, you know how old these cats are? Sixteen, man. You know what you can get for molesting kids?' Slowly her voice has risen in anger.

'I didn't molest anyone!' the man protests.

Shell turns to Manny. 'Did he molest you, Manny?'

'Yeah, man, in the parking lot,' Manny lies.

'That's not true!' Stuart cries.

'*How* did he molest you?' Cob's voice comes.

'Oh, uh, you know,' Manny tries to improvise. 'Like, you know, queer stuff.'

'That's a lie,' the man repeats wearily.

'No, man, I'm not fucking lying,' Manny tries to say what Shell and Cob want to hear.

'*How* did he molest you, Manny?' Cob insists.

'You know, man, like he put his hands all over my legs,' Manny says, 'and he . . .'

'No!' the man denies. 'And all of you know they're lies,' he realizes.

Suddenly Shell flashes the light on: Off! On! Now it remains lighted, an icy white pool enclosing Stuart.

'What else, Manny?' comes Cob's relentless questioning, pulling out of Manny the words they all know are untrue.

Manny frowns. Something strange is happening, *he's* being questioned. Again. And by her silence Shell is agreeing. 'Queer shit like that, man,' he says impatiently.

'Like what?' Cob insists.

'Like he touched my fucking prick, man!' Manny says heatedly.

'Did he take it out?' Cob insists.

'These are all lies! You know they're lies!' Stuart protests.

'Did he take it out, Manny?' Cob persists.

'Yeah, man!' Manny shouts. 'Then he wanted to bring me here to do more . . .'

Suddenly: 'You wanted to rape him!' Shell's fierce words at Stuart are both accusation and verdict.

'I just wanted to talk to him,' Stuart says guiltily, 'because he looked so lonesome standing out there.'

Lonesome! The word lashes at Manny. Intercepting the light, his shadow pounces on Stuart, he stands before the man. 'Fuck it if I'm lonesome, man!' he says angrily. 'I'm not shit-fucking lonesome! I got my friends, man!'

'Yeah, man, like he's got us . . . What else did he do, Manny?' Cob's voice comes hypnotically.

Jerry hears his own voice: 'He's already told you, Cob.'

'I want to hear it again,' Cob says darkly.

Shell glances quickly at Jerry, still standing. She shifts the light on him—the hint of an accusation. Then quickly she flashes it again on Stuart. She whistles. 'That's heavy shit Manny just laid on us about you, Stu,' she says. 'Manny's just a little dude, man; what if we told the pigs that you . . . ?'

'I'll tell them it's not true,' Stuart says firmly.

'They'll believe us,' Shell says with finality. 'Now why don't you sit down, Stu?' Her voice is almost kind. 'We're not going to hurt you; you're going to stay because you want to stay.'

'She promises we won't hurt you,' Jerry underscores, 'and we always keep our promises.' He wants to contain the violence, and yet allow the turbulent experience. Finally, he sits down on the floor. Manny sits too.

'Now sit down, Stu,' Shell's voice is still assuming the tone of kindness, but she holds the light firmly on him.

Body like ice, Stuart sits down.

'So, Stu,' Shell says, 'you were going to force Manny . . .'

Stuart interrupts urgently. 'No! He's the one who was standing there waiting to be approached.'

'I was just like digging the fucking fresh air, man!' Manny says indignantly. 'And you fucking came and propositioned me.'

'I wasn't going to *force* him!' Stuart defends.

'Look, man,' Shell says, 'what it's all about, like, is this cat here, Manny, when he was just . . .' Her voice stops abruptly. 'He was . . . molested . . . when he was . . .' Again her voice snags. Abruptly, her voice harsh: 'Tell us about yourself, Stu!' she commands.

Stuart grasps for anything that may thwart the relentless glare. 'I'm married,' he says desperately, 'I even have a boy; that's why I talked to Manny . . .' Immediately he knew he said the wrong thing.

'You're fucking married,' Shell is lashing, 'and you have a kid, and you . . . !'

Manny's words bolt: 'You bring your boyfriends to your house, you run your kid out?'

'Why are you torturing me?' Stuart says pitifully.

'To get into your head,' Jerry echoes, a new meanness churning. To attack life!

Now Shell can finish what she began earlier; her words rush; 'Like this cat here, man—Manny—like he was fucking molested when he was . . . eleven. He was molested by a man like you.' She's making up the story about Manny but suddenly her words tumble out with rage, her voice rising: 'When he was only eleven! And the creep jumped on him! On a little kid, a child!' Abruptly, she turns the light off, pulling down the darkness.

'No, man, it was Cob who was molested,' Manny begins to banter perversely. 'Like I remember, the creep tried to fucking rape you, Cob.'

In the darkness, Cob's face turns abruptly toward Manny.

'*Was* it you, Cob?' And Shell laughs, the tension—real or pretended—of the earlier moments snapping.

'Maybe it was *you*,' Cob says to her.

A black shadow over their seated bodies, Shell stands up

47

quickly. She breaks the electric current among them: 'Do you molest your own kid?' she thrusts savagely at Stuart. And again the blinding light shoots at him: On!

'I don't have a kid!' the man shouts back at her. 'I'm not even married . . .'

'Then you lied,' Shell accuses.

'Don't lie to us, man,' Cob warns.

'We're the four angels—and we don't dig lies.' Jerry forces out the words, deliberately overcoming pity.

'You ever been with a chick, Stu?' Cob's voice is steely.

'No,' the man admits wearily. Blinded by the harsh light, he hears only voices surrounding him menacingly.

'Diggit, man, the dude's never been with a chick!' Cob turns derisively to the others. 'Huccome, Stu? They scare you, man?'

'I just didn't want to,' the man avoids their stares.

Shell's light: Off!

'Why?' Cob badgers.

The light from a speeding car blazing through the crossed boards slashes the darkness like the blade of a guillotine.

'My mother . . .' Stuart blurts.

The darkness crashes on Jerry. He inhales deeply.

With shocking abruptness: 'What kind of a shit are you, blaming your mother for what you are?' Cob demands.

'I wasn't blaming her!' the man defends vehemently. 'I was just going to say she's the only woman I ever loved.'

Jerry stands up. He feels flushed, as if his head will explode. He stands by the window. The boards crossed before it create a trap. The void has been stirred—death is an electrified presence in it—he has to stop the empty whirling. By stirring another's torment? Always before, he felt another's panic—like now with Stuart. The death of his mother shattered his soul, that very vulnerability exposed him to the unfair slaughter. He must conquer the feelings that made him vulnerable, immunizing himself by becoming savage.

Sitting down again, Shell quickly changes the direction of the interrogation: 'Okay, Stu, so we're like trying to help you get into your head so you can get out of all the bad shit.' The flashlight: On!

'But you've got to tell us everything,' Cob says ominously.

'What do you want to know?' the man asks. To get into his head! So much of terror there. No! Suddenly he rushes again toward the door, to Escape into the dark corridor.

Cob grabs him.

Quickly Jerry is up, next to Stuart, both caught in the crystal web of Shell's light now. 'You promised you wouldn't hurt him,' Jerry reminds Cob. Then feeling the judgment of Shell's stare, he says, 'If you hit him, how the hell can we get into his head?'

Shell shifts the light away from Jerry; now he stands only in its peripheral glare.

'Let Stu go, Cob,' Shell says firmly.

Reluctantly, Cob releases Stuart.

Stuart stands in the white center.

Once again the four are sitting before him, like a terrible jury.

'When did you know you were queer?' Cob's words erupt.

Suddenly Shell whirls the light dizzily about the room, pulling objects starkly out of the thick darkness: a broken board, a shatter of glass on the floor, a crumbling piece of wall. Swiftly she drowns the man again in the glare of the lighted flashlight.

'Why the hell should I tell you?' Stuart resists.

'How old were you when you knew you were queer?' Cob persists.

Silence.

'Tell us,' Shell's voice is contained.

'Yeah, man,' Manny feels left out.

'I was your age,' Stuart says finally.

Silence.

'How did you know?' Cob's voice assaults coldly.

'I just did!' Stuart says.

'How!' Cob demands.

'I just . . . I was uncomfortable around girls . . . I . . . tried to force myself, but . . .' Now Stuart's body is unbearably hot, from the renewed awareness of the accumulated anxiety of years, the constant struggle.

To stop his own thoughts, to move from the edge of the fatal abyss which threatens him: the realization of aloneness, 'Speak up, man,' Jerry joins the interrogators. He's aware that Shell has turned, briefly, to face him, as if in welcome.

'I thought sex was dirty,' the man says dully.

'It is,' Shell says. Then she laughs.

'When did you first make it with a guy?' Cob addresses Stuart.

'I was your age,' the man answers.

Silence again.

Shell allows it to remain, stirring accusations, verdicts, sentences.

Cob breaks the silence: 'How did you know?'

'Why are you torturing me?' the man repeats.

'How did you first make it?' comes Cob's voice.

'I . . .' Stuart is terrified of Cob. If he answers, will they leave him alone? stop stirring the crushing guilt? Guilt . . . The pattern of his life: desire, fear, guilt. And he's shattered by the enormous truth. Even now, trapped in this unbudging nightmare, even now he feels an overwhelming desire, acutely aware of the bodies of the three youngmen surrounding him.

'Was the guy you made it with, was he older than you?' Shell asks. 'Did he force you?' Then her voice shouts: 'You didn't even know what the hell was happening, did you, Stu? He just grabbed you!' The flashlight: Off!

'Yes!' Stuart lies, to enlist her as an ally—something in her voice . . .

Shell's tense body relaxes in the darkness; she seems somewhat diminished. Then she accuses: 'You're lying.' And the light pounces on him again.

'Yes,' the man admits. 'I wasn't forced.'

'Did you force him?' Cob asks.

'I've never forced anyone,' Stuart says quietly.

'You were going to force Manny,' Shell says.

'I wasn't going to force him,' Stuart says tiredly. 'I really thought—I really did—that he wanted . . . me, too.'

'*Shit*, man!' Manny is enraged. 'What the fuck made you fucking think I wanted a fucking queer? What the fuck made you think I fucking wanted *you*, man! You mean you thought I was a . . .'

'No,' the man says. 'I just hoped that . . .'

'I'm no fucking fag, man!' Manny is furious.

'I'm sure you're not,' Stuart says dully.

'Okay,' Manny composes himself.

'How did you make it with guys? How!' Cob's voice shoots.

'How many times, how many times, how many times?' Manny parodies, seized suddenly by laughter. 'Just like a hung-up priest at confession.' His anger shifts to Cob; he resents Cob's seizing what was to be his interrogation.

'You fucking shut up, man!' Cob warns him.

'How? Many? Times?' Manny repeats with taunting slowness.

'I don't know how many times,' the man says vaguely.

'That's not what I fucking asked,' Cob reminds. 'I asked you *how* you made it.'

'I'm not going to tell you a goddamn thing!' Stuart rebels. 'Why the hell don't you find out for yourself if you're so interested?'

Instantly Cob is standing before him, his enlarged shadow engulfing Stuart. 'Yes, you fucking are going to tell us!'

'I blew him!' Stuart shouts, and he stares at Cob's thighs before him.

'And what else?' Cob proceeds relentlessly.

'That's all,' Stuart says quietly.

'What else!' Cob demands.

'That's all!' Stuart shouts.

'How many times, how many times?' Manny is convulsed.

51

Then: silence, accumulating. The house is invaded by its deafening sounds.

Cob's world: flashes of black; discordant sounds.

Now Manny stands up, to wrest the interrogation back to himself as leader. 'Like we're gonna lay some righteous help on your head, Stu,' he says.

Shell frowns.

Jerry looks at her. Her hair is luminous even in the dark. When this night is ended . . . ?

'How?' the man says. A recurrent wave of desire engulfs him. His thoughts rush crazily: Might it all somehow turn out all right? Futilely trying to order the horror, his mind explodes in sexual images.

'What the fuck are you into, man?' Cob asks Manny.

'It's *my* fucking interrogation,' Manny asserts himself tensely. '*I'm* the dude who got fucked over and interrogated in the J.D. home—not you!' He says to Stuart: 'Diggit, man, like we're gonna make you straight.'

Shell's light slashes the room fiercely.

6

In that shaft of shifting light, Jerry sees a dead bird trapped in the transom of the old house. Had it been trying to Escape the wind? His mother hadn't wanted to die, either. Desperately he had tried to breathe his life into her, pushing his breath into her no-longer-moving lips. Where is she now? . . . He sees Shell, Cob, Manny. He feels their meanness, and his: revolt against life which contains death.

The angry whirl of Shell's flashlight—was it meant to warn Manny? If so, he won't retreat: 'Like you said you've never been with a chick, Stu,' he goes on; 'well, you're gonna be with one now.'

Cob stands in the shadows, as if preparing to choose sides in a quickly shaping game.

Jerry understands with resentment: Manny is going to taunt Stuart with Shell. He moves slightly toward her.

Shell turns off the flashlight with finality.

In the tense darkness Manny moves toward her—and he takes the flashlight from her; he's relieved that she didn't protest. Now he crouches near Stuart. Suddenly, whirling about like a gunfighter, he flashes the light on Shell: 'Pow!'

'What the hell!' Shell protests.

'You did it to *us*,' Manny reminds her.

Not blinking, Shell looks defiantly at Manny.

The terror multiplies. Stuart knows he may become a mere object in a struggle among the four.

'Isn't she outasite?' Manny asks Stuart.

'Yes,' the man whispers.

53

Shell's yellow eyes are frozen in the light.

How far will she allow Manny to go? Jerry looks at Shell.

As if in answer, suddenly she leans back on the floor, her breasts flare full and lovely. She smiles radiantly. Is she playing along with Manny?

Now the shadow of Cob stands behind Shell. Yes, they're into Manny's game. 'Diggit, Stu; isn't she like fine, man?' Cob asks.

Jerry moves closer to Shell, joining them. He touches her hair, barely. He hears himself say: 'You dig her, Stu?'

The flashlight still bathes her, Cob and Jerry are opaque shadows in the peripheral light.

Stuart doesn't answer.

Rashly Jerry bends over Shell, his fingers glide along her throat, lightly touching her shoulders. She allows the gesture. To taunt Stuart—only for that reason? Suddenly her body stiffens. Quickly, Jerry withdraws his fingers. Her flesh was cold.

In the fleeting light of a vagrant car, Cob's sunglassed eyes flash like angry bulbs. 'You want her, Stu?' he seizes the direction of the game. 'And then you won't be queer any more.'

'I'd . . . rather . . . not . . .' the man whispers.

Cob reacts in faked outrage. 'Don't you like her, man?'

'She's very beautiful,' Stuart says quickly.

Feeling pleased with his tactic, 'Give it a try, man,' Manny says.

'Move over here, Stuart,' Cob orders.

Manny turns angrily to Cob; Cob is grabbing control. And what the hell? Manny thinks. It was to be his interrogation; he's tougher than they are—he's been busted; he's even done time in the state institution; they haven't. He shoots the light at Cob, as if in ambiguous warning.

'On Stuart!' Cob demands. The purple gaze is electric in the light.

Responding automatically to his command, Manny shifts the light back to Stuart.

Stuart has not moved.

54

'I said, move over here,' Cob barks at him.

Stuart moves toward Cob, toward Shell.

Shell stands quickly. Will she retreat?

'Kneel!' Cob orders Stuart. 'Like you've knelt before dudes!'

Suddenly Shell's body is rigid, as if she must force it not to retreat.

'Oooo-eee,' Manny giggles.

Cob pushes Stuart to kneel. And now he places his hand firmly on the man's head as if to force it against Shell's legs.

Instantly, Shell moves away. Then she laughs. Manny begins to laugh, too—and then Jerry, in relief. Their laughter envelops Stuart. Frantically, hysterically, he joins their laughter.

Only Cob is not laughing. He's standing before the kneeling form of Stuart.

His laughter choking, Stuart stares at Cob's spread legs. Desire erupts.

Cob pushes him backward on the floor. 'Sick fucking *queer*!' he shouts.

'You promised you wouldn't hurt him,' Jerry reminds him.

Stuart recovers quickly, stands. 'I'm getting out of here!' he gasps hysterically. 'And don't try to stop me!'

Manny flashes the light on Stuart as he moves: a relentless searchlight refusing to release him. 'We'll call the pigs and tell them you were molesting us,' Manny reminds. 'Remember, man, we're just little kids.'

Stuart shouts his accusation at them: 'Kids!—yes!—but your cruelty is . . .' He shakes his head wearily. 'You're not even kids—you're old with cruelty.'

Cruelty. Jerry feels lacerated by the accusation. Cruelty.

'Stu's hysterical, he needs a smoke,' Shell says easily.

Trying to breathe evenly—but gasping—the man nods eagerly. Just the lighting of a cigarette will provide a pause to contain and order the still-shapeless terror.

Shell brings forth a pack of cigarettes, gives one to Stuart, lights it carefully for him.

The man inhales.

Shell watches him closely as he smokes within the still-glaring light.

The others watch her.

Now the man is aware of the intense stares.

Shell's voice is ice: 'Guess what I put on the tip of your cigarette, Stu?'

The man looks down at the cigarette in bewilderment.

'Go on, guess,' Shell insists.

Cruelty. The word floats on Jerry's mind. The force that seized his mother into death, that was the ultimate cruelty. And his vulnerability—weakness, he renames it—prepared him for the horror. To be strong! Yet . . . Cruelty . . .

'What!' the man blurts.

'Acid, I put acid on the tip of your cigarette,' Shell says.

'What kind of acid?' the man asks uncertainly, the fear hasn't yet shaped.

'LSD,' Shell pronounces.

'Far out!' Manny giggles.

Terror springs on the man. 'What will it do to me!'

'Well, uh,' Cob comes in, 'like if you let yourself, you'll dig it.' His voice changes abruptly. 'As uptight as you are, you'll probably freak—and end up in the psycho ward for days or even months.'

A frantic trapped animal, 'Don't stop me from getting out of here!' Stuart yells.

'Where will you go?' Shell asks coldly. 'It'll start coming on you like in about half an hour and it's powerful shit.' She raises her hands—enlarged by the light into monstrous shadows, giant claws—as if to lunge at him like the drug. 'Like it really *comes* at you!'

'I couldn't have taken that much on the tip of that cigarette!' the man is arguing with his fear.

'All it takes is like a lick of the tongue,' Manny says. 'Now why don't you just groove on it?'

Jerry watches in horror. And new fascination. He looks at Shell. So at ease with cruelty. And so, nothing can hurt *her*.

56

She's immunized herself; she can't feel pain like his.

Stuart gags, attempting to spit out whatever has invaded his system. 'I'm afraid!'

'You'll bum yourself out for sure,' Cob shakes his head.

Violent nausea, dizziness. The man staggers to the door. The light held by Manny pursues him. Now Stuart is rushing along the dark enclosing corridor. He's at the window. He imagines their hands on him, pulling him back like savages into the darkness. But already he's climbing out of the window, the house.

'The dude's gonna bum for sure!' Cob says.

'It wasn't acid,' Shell says quietly. 'I didn't put anything on the cigarette.'

Cob laughs, Manny giggles.

Suddenly Jerry is running along the corridor. He's already climbed through the window; he's rushing away from the house.

The others follow him hurriedly, but they stop at the window.

'Where the hell is he going?' Manny asks.

'He's fucking scared, he's running away from us!' Cob says, almost victoriously.

'No,' Shell says decisively.

From the window they watch Jerry with Stuart; Stuart is retching violently in the parking lot.

'He's just going to tell him it wasn't acid,' Shell says easily. 'He's still weak.'

In the car lot. 'They were putting you on; there was nothing on the cigarette!' Jerry is yelling at Stuart.

Wearily, Stuart straightens up. 'You're sure?' he asks in vast relief.

'I'm sure,' Jerry says.

Stuart actually reaches out to touch Jerry on the arm. To him —despite all the terror they exposed him to—to him, at this moment, standing as he is in the halo of a street light, Jerry looks like a lost, beautiful angel. 'Thank you,' Stuart utters.

Jerry returns quickly to the dark corridor. He faces the three.

'If he'd gone to the cops or the hospital, they would come looking for us,' he says hurriedly. He's trying to tell them that he did not really surrender to pity. But he knows he did.

'Sure,' Shell says tersely.

'Sure,' Cob echoes darkly.

'Fuck it,' Manny says, imitating Shell's disappointment earlier over the escaped voyeur.

For moments they stand in the silent darkness. Gone, Stuart has left an almost palpable emptiness. Without his terror, they must look elsewhere.

'Now what?' Cob asks. Again the wasteland of empty time, stretching.

'Let's do some more dope,' Manny says. It might execute time.

'It's all gone,' Shell says flatly.

'We could go get some more from that dude near the river,' Manny insists. He feels suddenly sad. Stuart's borrowed reality lingers—and the dope may pull them away from it.

'I'd dig some acid,' Cob approves.

They pronounce words. It's as if the confrontation with Stuart has left them diminished because there was no real climax for them.

For Jerry the night stretches emptily too. Yet a disturbing, disturbed part of him was filled by the mean encounter—his initiation away from vulnerability and tears? Within the whirling void, a stasis was provided by the unresolved violence. Yes, Stuart's terror freed him momentarily from his own. Now he pulls away from the newly haunting memory of Stuart.

'*You* want some acid?' Shell asks Jerry abruptly.

Deliberately cool—to match their cool—he shrugs.

'It'll clear your head,' Shell tells him.

Her voice seems curiously gentle to Jerry. Seems? Through some particular horror of her own—but what?—does she understand the wailing emptiness? . . . The proffered drug. To clear his head, she said. Perhaps it will be the door to his salvation. At least a substitute for salvation.

They stand outside now under the star-punctured sky. A breeze suddenly becomes a nervous gust. An augur of the desolate wind, rising again? In moments will an army of tumbleweeds invade the city from the desert? Already those crushed against the house stir restlessly.

Again Cob chooses to drive, Shell lets him—and again she sits in back with Jerry. To be with him, or to affront Cob? The question is important to Jerry as they speed away on the freeway.

They exit on the Mesa highway and into the outskirts of the city draped in the shadows of thick trees. Traveling on a dirt road now, they reach a torn-down shack near the Rio Grande. Cardboards are tacked against its smashed windows to keep out the wind. Leprous weeds cover the otherwise bare lawn. Several cars, some partly stripped and propped like mechanical skeletons on bricks, are parked before it, or abandoned there. Rock music wafts the dark country air.

Cob knocks loudly to be heard.

A curtain parts at the window, a face peers out, the curtains close again carefully, the door opens.

Inside, the room is dimly lit. Gradually faces float eerily out of the light, which is the dyed color of koolade. At least a dozen long-haired youngmen and girls sit on the floor.

Slightly apart, two girls huddle against the wall and over a sheet of paper. One is frailly blond, almost translucent. The other is delicately Oriental.

Shell, Cob, and Manny join the circle on the floor. Immediately someone hands Shell a number, which she smokes, passes to the others. The joint of weed, passing slowly and silently—and another is instantly started, moving in the opposite direction—binds them intimately as it goes from hand to mouth to hand in the familiar ritual.

Shell holds up the number to Jerry, who stands. He hits from it, expecting nothing from it now, getting nothing. Then he turns to the two girls outside the circle.

The two are making slow, careful, graceful water-color marks with brushes on a sheet of paper. Colors meld, creating

59

quivering electric edges. The two seem deliberately isolated from the others—perhaps that's why Jerry turned to them.

He hands the number to the frail blond girl. She seems to be protected by fragile crystalline glass. She inhales, passes the joint to the other girl.

'You like colors?' the Oriental girl asks Jerry softly.

'Yes,' he answers.

The blond girl lifts the drawing dreamily. The colors run in clashing streaks, creating a flood of vari-colored waves. She holds it up to Jerry.

'Sound,' she says. 'It's a picture of sound.'

'And this is a picture of God,' the Oriental girl says. She holds up another drawing: a sheet covered with shades of blue like overlapping wings.

'Gentle, like that,' says the blond girl. 'That's God.'

Jerry reaches abruptly for the drawing. He stares angrily at it. 'I think it's weird—really weird and ugly—and it's all crazy.'

7

This time Shell drove. Manny sits aggressively in front with her.

'Can't you go any faster?' Cob taunts Shell. 'Are you too stoned to drive?'

'Shit,' Manny defends, 'Shell can drive ripped any fucking time.'

'What's putting you uptight?' Shell aims at Cob. 'I can't fucking help it if the cat was out of good dope.'

Cob shifts his disappointment to anger: 'Let's go to Jerry's big pad.' For him, the house Jerry has not let them into is looming as a symbol of the new-angel's unapproachable distance—and it affronts him.

Jerry says nothing. But his resolve grows that they won't—that no one will—invade that part of his life. He regrets even having told them that he locked his mother's room.

Shell is silent.

'Why don't you want us in your house?' Cob verbalizes the accusation.

Jerry says: 'The cats aren't used to strangers.' Then in a very quiet voice: 'They miss my mother.' Yes, and they seem lost, lost like him . . . The brown Burmese waiting before the closed room—he remembers her especially: the bewildered, angry yellow eyes. If he could explain to her! But even he doesn't 'understand'. How could he—how could anyone—explain death?—suddenly an invisible constant in his life.

'We'll go to The Seed,' Shell again releases Jerry from Cob's scrutiny.

'There's always good shit there!' Manny extols.

Immediately, the announcement of a design lifts the brooding heaviness threatening them. They've vanquished another inch of time.

Soon, rushing there as if to outspeed their thoughts before they form, they're in Anapra, a small town in New Mexico, just minutes outside of El Paso. A town more like a village, it's an awkward, ugly conglomeration of adobe houses in which poor Chicanos live. The streets are cloudy with dust. On a tall mountain dominating the village is an awesome, giant statue of Christ; a strong, stone, primitive Jesus with arms outstretched. Railroad tracks tangle like angry snakes at the foot of the mountain, and the Rio Grande meanders casually past a small bridge, on which, on hot evenings, restless young Chicanos stand waiting sullenly for nothing. There's an ironic scattering of nightclubs in the village—and a disdainful racetrack. And on a filthy street, more like a field of dirt than a street, is The Seed—a doper hangout: a square, squat, flimsy building like an abandoned barn. Beer, wine, soft drinks are sold inside. Outside, a ragged camp of young hippy gypsies exchange dope openly.

Shell parks among the many cars situated in studied disorder. The four get out. Here and there, other young people cluster in dark cars, the light from a number occasionally flickering like a lazy firefly in the darkness. Long-haired youngmen and girls mill idly, some sit or lie stoned on the dirt like the remnants of a crushed, resigned army.

Inside, wooden tables, booths are gathered tightly at one side, allowing a cleared area for dancing. Against the wall, screens, like giant sheets, are propped, awaiting the attack of colors of a light show. Already two long-haired youngish men hover in a small coop before the patched screens, arranging the whirling discs that will project the bursting lights. To one side of the screens is a small elevated platform. Sequined drums glistening red, white, and blue dominate the stage, a youngman hovers over them ready to perform another precise ritual.

There are perhaps a hundred people here tonight—more

62

than that outside. Some are shirtless, barefoot, all wear bright colors. Cool, slender young bodies, they seem to move within private glass chambers, enclosed but highly visible to each other. In isolated display.

The four sit at a table, one of them occasionally nodding to someone familiar nearby.

All here seem merely to be waiting. Just waiting. For the music to begin? For the light show to flash? For something else? For nothing? There's a stoned silence, a lack of movement, as if only the music may commit the young bodies to motion. A wake at which the corpse, delayed, will be young.

Now the band of five youngmen—faces intense, transfixed—has begun its subterranean sounds of pulsing, tortured climaxes. Suddenly amplifiers seize the thundering sound, thrust it out even louder, blaring. The room itself vibrates. And there's the wailing orgasmic voice of the lead singer; at his feet a tattered groupie like a sad rag doll. The sounds shatter the stoned trance like light on glass. Here and there a shirtless youngman moves his head back and forth, a barefoot girl comes to life. A flooding river of sound—opposing waves crashing in spellbinding cacophony—the deafening, mesmerizing rhythm is a physical presence in total control of the enclosed glass worlds of the stoned young people . . . Jerry feels a surging release, and a heavy sorrow, as if the music contains both.

Now, as if spewed out by the music itself, colors flash on the screens from the whirling disc before the projector. Orange! Blue! Red! Purple! Green! Yellow! Within the erupting colors, bodies captured by them seem to burn, melt, freeze, thaw, in a purgatory of colors and sound.

As if her body had been suddenly charged by the electric vibrations of light and music, Shell stands. She holds her hands out before her. To Jerry? To Manny? To Cob? Quickly Cob rises. Separately, he and Shell move into the clearing on the floor, two shadows thrust starkly into the spinning colors.

Colors exploding like rockets on them, Shell and Cob dance. Motion itself, Shell's body twists, arches sensually, her long,

long hair lashes ferociously like an angry whip. In the shifting colors, she seems to move in rhythmic jerks without transition.

His movements slower, more deliberate, Cob is a dark form occasionally set ablaze by colored lights. To the cruel rhythm, his hands move fiercely before him as if confronting an enemy. Thrusting, lowering itself, his body arches from the hips.

More than a dance, it seems to be a violent test to see how far each can get from the other—and still be close, still together: sharing only the colored lightning on the screens and the throbbing currents of sound. Slowly, the two move farther and farther from each other, gyrating, flailing savagely, within their invisible cages.

Now slides replace the colors on the screen. A blue heart! A red butterfly! A vibrating black flower! . . . A luminous orange angel! The slide is held: the angel's wings seem about to encompass—to embrace or trap—the shabby barn.

Jerry remembers: The avenging angel in church. The screaming, unrepentant dragon.

Manny shakes his head. 'That Shell—man . . . She's . . . far out.' He closes his eyes—as if to seal within his mind whatever images flashed there.

As if alternately seized and released by an electric current, Shell's body becomes rigid, relaxes, becomes rigid, loosens. She holds one hand before her thighs . . . Facing her, Cob's body trembles in a paroxysm of motion; and his hand too dangles between his legs.

Then the music stops! The colors, the slides disappear! In the gray-yellowish light which remains, Cob and Shell stand facing each other for moments. Then—separately, quickly— they return to the table.

'Let's split,' Shell says suddenly.

Soundlessly they rise.

Outside, youngmen and girls waiting in the night offer them grass. But Shell moves away from the milling groups. Now she's talking, alone, to a youngman wearing an Indian headband. He disappears momentarily, into an old van painted with

64

blazing stars; he returns, hands Shell a packet. With a smile she holds out the packet to the three waiting for her nearby.

'Pow!' Manny approves.

Shell gets into the driver's side of the car, Jerry gets in front.

The Texas night is still. Dust pursues the car from the unpaved dirt road. There is no moon. But the stars are luminous silver.

'We'll go back to that empty house,' Shell announces.

'And do the acid!' Cob says.

'We've never tripped at night,' Manny says excitedly.

'We're not tripping till tomorrow,' Shell says.

'Why the fuck not?' Cob asserts himself.

Shell smiles: 'Would you dig some cocaine tonight?'

'Cocaine!' Cob blurts. 'You got cocaine?'

'Yes,' Shell says.

'Pow!' Manny repeats.

In the distance a siren wails. Forlornly. Jerry remembers: the ambulance. Will the new drug fill the void? he wonders. Or will it be like the grass, the hash? Nothing.

They've reached the dark, boarded-up house by the bar; the brooding house is harshly real in the fantastic night. Shell parks in the familiar alley. They get out. Shell carries the packet she got outside The Seed, Manny carries the flashlight, Cob carries the transistor radio, not on. Before the window they use for an entrance, they pause. The loose boards are parted. Cob's wolfish face registers, alert.

Inside: along the dark corridor: suddenly: 'Cool it, there's someone else in here!' Cob whispers excitedly.

'Maybe Stuart came back,' Manny says with apprehension.

'No,' Cob dismisses definitely.

From the inner darkness: stirrings. A long sigh.

'Maybe Stuart brought the pigs . . .' Manny begins.

'Keep your voice down!' Cob orders. 'It's not Stuart.' Quickly he takes the flashlight from Manny, giving him the radio.

They walk silently along the dark corridor, Cob clearly leading them this time.

The same sounds again, increasing. Now: a sudden gasp.

Cob stops abruptly at the door to the room where they interrogated Stuart. A car's light wounds the darkness, revealing in a bright flash like a quickly focused slide, two male bodies fused into one, one stooped over, the other entering him from behind, pants and shorts at their feet.

Shell's world: A sudden blackness . . . Automatically she turns away quickly. Instinctively, seized by the emanating waves of vagrant sexuality, Jerry reaches for her arm. To touch her? To keep her here? His fingers quickly slide down to her hand. It's cold. She doesn't withdraw it.

Cob floods the two men in light.

Two stunned faces turn. The youngman being fucked begins to straighten up, the second to pull his prick out of the other.

Cob's voice shoots through the darkness: 'Stay exactly like you are, you weird motherfuckers!'

'The cops!' the youngman penetrating the other blurts.

'Oh, God, no!' the second youngman moans. He begins to reach for his pants.

'I said don't move!' Cob commands. He advances, holding the harsh light like a rifle.

Frozen in terror, the two bodies remain fused, the one's cock softening instantly against the other.

'Finish what you were doing—queers!' Cob says.

'Please . . .' the second of the two whimpers.

'Let us go!' pleads the other.

'Don't stand up! Don't move. I'm warning you two creeps: finish!' Cob fires.

The others stand at the door. Still touching—barely touching —Shell's hand, Jerry stares at the two—and then away, at Shell.

A tide of giggles issues from Manny's mouth nervously: 'They're *fucking*!' he blurts.

66

Composed now—pulling defiantly at composure—Shell's voice rips: *'Finish!'*

Jerry pulls away his fingers from her cold, cold hand.

'We can't . . .' the first youngman whimpers.

'If you let us go . . .' the second starts.

The two see only threatening shadows clustered about the door. Terror has quickly replaced sexual excitement. The light advances menacingly in a bright crystal circle.

'Finish, motherfuckers!' Cob says darkly.

'Do what he says!' Shell deliberately matches Cob. But she's looking away from the two, at Cob.

His prick still against the other, but soft, the terrified youngman presses against the other's buttocks.

'Ooo-eeeee—they're fucking,' Manny giggles nervously.

Jerry merely waits, as if for a definite reaction to the bewildering sexual spectacle.

Cob advances closer to the two youngmen. 'Fuck him!' his voice thunders at the youngman in back of the other.

'I can't!' he whimpers.

'Go on!' Shell demands angrily.

Desperate to end the sexual charade—to pacify them—the youngman grinds against the other's buttocks, but his soft prick cannot penetrate. He merely pushes against the other, who whimpers in fear.

Suddenly Cob drops the flashlight to his side, its light spills on the rotting floor.

The soothing semi-darkness embraces the two youngmen. Quickly, they straighten up, adjust their clothes. Tensely, they face the four shadows. 'What do you want?' says the first youngman.

'We're pigs, man!' Manny says. 'And we're going to fucking bust you for doing queer shit.' He pauses. 'Let's interrogate *them!*'

'No,' Cob rejects decisively. 'Split!' he commands the two. 'I'll count to three . . . One!'

The two stumble past them.

'Like animals,' Cob's words shoot out in accusation.

'Man, we really freaked them out,' Manny says.

'Animals!' Cob yells after the two.

'Animals!' Shell seizes the word, laughing harshly.
'Animals!'

'Animals!' Manny joins them.

'Animals . . .' Jerry echoes softly. But to whom is he
addressing the word? He feels relief that his own violent
excitement—and it had been stirred by the charged anger—has
ebbed.

'We shoulda fucking interrogated them!' Manny insists.
'Why didn't you wanna?' he questions Cob.

Cob doesn't answer. The flashlight is still at his side.

Shell sits on the decaying wooden floor. The others join her,
slowly. She turns on the transistor radio. Rock sounds float like
soft magic into the darkness.

'Let's do the dope now!' Manny says; he wants release from
the tension.

Shell's voice comes coldly, unexpectedly: 'Not yet. Let
Jerry suggest something,' she says.

'Right on,' Cob agrees. He lays the lighted flashlight on the
floor: a shaft of light exposing each splinter on the floor,
enlarging it grotesquely.

'They want you to make up a game, man,' Manny says, somewhat bewildered, to Jerry.

'You've just like come along with us so far,' Shell says.

Why is she turning against him—because he touched her
and she allowed it? Jerry wonders. Because he touched her cold,
cold hand?

'And you blew the scene with Stuart,' Cob accuses him.

'Maybe he could make up a game about locked rooms. Or
death,' come Shell's brutal words. Grabbing it quickly from the
floor, she flashes the light on the transom. On the dead bird
caught there.

Death: Jerry looks up at the crushed bird. Then at Shell in
overt accusation. She's deliberately stirring the black sorrow he

thought only earlier she understood, might try to calm. Angered and confused, he stands up quickly, to leave.

Whether because of that or because that phase of cruelty has been run through, Shell withdraws abruptly. She pulls the light away from the transom. She places the flashlight again on the floor—a sheet of lighted transparent ice. 'Let's do the cocaine,' she says quickly.

Jerry still doesn't sit down.

'Come on, man, join us,' Shell says. 'We were just putting you on—you're one of us, man.'

But is he? And does he finally want to be? Still, Jerry remains apart. Yet, if he leaves . . . Alone . . . Night contains death. And this thought intrudes powerfully: to vanquish Shell's cruelty . . .

She's smiling radiantly at him.

Now she brings out a small plastic bag containing a thin white powder like talcum. With intense attention, she spreads it on a piece of paper on the floor. Using a small strip of cardboard as a knife, she divides the powder into four neat, thin rows on the paper. Then she rolls a dollar bill thinly, like a slender cigarette.

'You cover one side of your nose like this,' she explains, doing it. 'And you bring the bill to the other, and then you bring the tip of it to the shit, and you snort the hell out of it and hold it. Like this . . .' She bends over the powder, inhales forcefully. The first rail of white powder disappears. She leans back, closes her eyes. 'Wow!'

Jerry sits down with them, lured by the prospect.

Cob reaches eagerly for the rolled dollar bill.

'Don't exhale till you've got it all in,' Shell tells him.

'I know how to snort the son of a bitch,' Cob says. He takes the powder expertly. Now he too leans back, eyes closed, welcoming the rush.

Manny does it clumsily, blowing bits of the powder over the paper, so that he has to snort all over it. He inhales loudly. It hits him. 'Pow! Outasite!'

The shielded purple-glassed look issuing a challenge to him, Cob hands the bill to Jerry.

Quickly Jerry takes the bill, leans over the powder, inhales. Immediately he felt a tickling in his nose, then a sudden deadening. And then: a violent, decreasingly violent, numbing, beautiful sensation, like a lingering blue rush.

8

Standing up suddenly, Jerry deliberately separates himself from the others. Will it last? this racing feeling of power and release?

Abandoned in their violated circle, the others look sad to him, sitting close to each other but not touching. Sad and isolated. Like unwanted children. Yet the drug has created a superficial closeness. But paradoxically a wall, too.

Shell looks up at Jerry. 'How do you feel?'

He sits down again. He doesn't answer. But, yes, this time he's reacting to the drug, he knows with relief. He merely nods at Shell. His body seems to be rushing frantically—speeding without motion. Then he hears his own words: 'Poor Stuart, man.'

'What is this, man?' Cob says.

'Jerry's our conscience,' Shell says softly. 'Or maybe we're really his.'

'Yeah, ole Stuart,' Manny says. 'Hell, he wasn't such fucking bad people.'

'He just wanted to bugger your ass,' Cob says.

'No, he didn't,' Manny says with conviction. 'He was just like lonesome.'

Lonesome.

Silence.

And within that crush of lonesome silence, Jerry sees: Strange children in the dark house. He laughs uncontrollably.

'It's far out, isn't it, man?' Manny asks.

'Yeah,' Jerry agrees.

'What is?' Cob asks, smiling.

'Suddenly I just saw it,' Jerry says. 'Like we're really children.'

'We are,' Manny mutters. 'We're the little people.'

'I was a child,' Shell sighs. Her sudden laughter smashes the words she just spoke.

Cob echoes her sigh, then her abrupt laughter.

Then silence rocked softly by the radio's mellow sounds.

Silence. And the drugged music. And time—this moment of time—conquered.

Manny shakes his head dazedly. 'Can you diggit, man? Those two dudes, screwing!' His mind opens on the earlier scene, springs to another : 'Ole Stuart . . .'

More silence.

Time.

The rushing stoned magic wanes.

Jerry feels a heavy disappointment that it lasted so briefly, the sensation of speed, eroding pain.

Cob tries to cling to it : 'Let's do the acid now,' he says.

'No, man,' Shell says. 'Tomorrow. There's got to be something for tomorrow.'

Abruptly she gets up. By tacit agreement they know they're ending the night. But Cob remains sitting, as if he dare not yet commit himself to the knowledge of its end. Soon there will be tomorrow to fill, the thought hovers over him.

To Jerry, Cob looks totally isolated sitting there by himself as if determined to stretch the moments of superficial intimacy.

When the others begin to move out of the room, Cob looks about him in bewilderment. His world, shadows. Quickly, like a child afraid of the dark, he follows them out of the house.

Cob in front with her, Shell drives swiftly in deep silence.

They're at Manny's. Before the shabby house, Manny gets out. 'Later—tomorrow,' he says eagerly, as if that prospect makes the entrance into his own house bearable.

Before they drive away, they hear a woman's badgering voice.

Shell, Cob, Jerry. All in front.

Then Cob realizes with resentment that Shell is going to

drive him home first. Already they're in his neighborhood, a middle-class cluster of houses. Already Shell is stopped before his house,

Jerry is relieved he'll be alone with her.

Cob's house is lighted inside.

Cob blurts bitterly: 'They're still up, my mother . . . and her. They stay real late . . .' His hand grips the door as if to postpone something inevitable and terrible. Then he says incongruously: 'Some day I'd like to do so much dope I'd fucking get so fucked up—so ripped and messed that I'd just wander all over the fucking world and get lost and not even know who I fucking am!'

'There isn't enough dope in the world to do that,' Shell says soberly. Quickly: 'I'll pick you up tomorrow morning,' she tells him, as if to break his abrupt intensity.

And she did. Defiantly Cob opens the door of the car, gets out. He adjusts the purple glasses like a protective shield before his face.

Advancing toward what? Jerry stares after Cob. And so the drug left them exactly where they were before. His disappointment grows.

Shell drives away quickly.

Jerry, Shell. Alone. The moment when he brushed her arm, barely touched her hand in the dark house—he remembers that out of the night's experience now. He tries to forget the other incidents and the coldness of her flesh.

'Cob can't stand his sister,' Shell tells him. 'And he's so bummed out over it that it hangs him up.' Then she blurts bluntly: 'Like you about your mother.'

The awareness of being alone with Shell shatters into the stunning awareness of loss and death—love smeared by death. 'Suddenly she's not here,' he says in wonder, the recurring amazement of each moment's awareness. Absence has physical dimensions.

'You can't let it bring you down,' Shell says, her voice so controlled it comes as a whisper.

Again, he has the feeling that she understands, that she wants to bring him out of the black void. But what can she know of such loss? No loss in the world equaled it.

'Once you say "No," it's okay!' Shell says.

'How the hell can you say no to death?' Jerry asks angrily.

'By being strong—then nothing can bring you down,' Shell says.

'By torturing others?' Jerry hears himself say.

'We didn't torture anybody,' Shell says firmly.

Jerry looks at her in surprise. Stuart's terrified face haunts him.

Shell's voice is commanding: 'We didn't fucking torture anyone,' she repeats.

'I thought that's what you wanted,' Jerry says in genuine surprise.

'No!' she says forcefully.

'Then what was it all about with Stuart, Shell?' Jerry asks.

'Getting strong,' she answers immediately. 'Us *and* him! *He'll* be stronger, next time he won't . . .' She stops abruptly. She looks at him intently. They've reached his sister's house. 'You need us,' she tells him unexpectedly.

He stares back at her. Does *she* need us? he wonders. The smile on her face stirs echoes of the night's cruelty. Does she really believe she helped Stuart? Or, the thought shatters Jerry, is this her way of getting to him, into *his* head? Is he part of her search for frantic experience? I won't be, he tells himself. He answers her finally. 'Maybe, maybe not.'

She laughs. Released by her laughter, he laughs too, mirthlessly. Their laughter is forced, forlorn.

'Okay, so we put each other on,' she says, as if to obliterate all seriousness.

'Yeah.' Jerry accepts the release.

'Tomorrow?' she says.

He wants to break through her shield, to pay her back for her flashing cruelty—and to touch her. 'Okay,' he agrees.

74

'And don't eat breakfast!' she calls after him. 'You've got to be pure for the acid.'

Jerry hears the roar of her departing car. Tomorrow.

He goes into the dark house. His sister is asleep.

Tomorrow.

He falls asleep listening to the soft sounds of the radio, and Creedence Clearwater Revival singing:

> 'Someone told me long ago
> There's a calm before the storm
> I know
> I've been waiting for too long
> I wanna know
> Have you ever seen the rain?'

He woke to the news on the radio, he turns it off quickly. Immediately—the black awareness of death. He dresses hurriedly. His sister is gone—there's a note. He rushes out of the house, anxious. Yes! he needs them!

It's a clear, pure, azure day.

He sees Shell's car approaching. Instantly he feels let down. Manny is already with her and he had looked forward to being with her alone again even for the moments before they picked the others up. Greeting the two, he doesn't let them know he's disappointed; but he sits alone in back.

Before Cob's house a feline young woman of twenty stares at them.

'That's Janet, Cob's sister,' Manny explains. 'He really hates her.'

Shell blares the horn.

The youngwoman looks directly at her, smiling; there's a trace of challenge in the smile.

Shell doesn't glance at her.

Now Cob rushes out of the house. He doesn't acknowledge the youngwoman, who only smiles harder at Shell.

In the car Cob is very quiet behind the shield of sunglasses.

Then his anger erupts. 'Fuck it if I go to work so Janet can go back to school! . . . My old lady, man, she laid down that she fucking expects *me* to get a job the rest of the summer. But Janet can sit on her ass all day. Fuck them!'

They drive silently, accepting Cob's outrage; driving on Mesa toward the desert, which gleams white in the gold heat and azure sky.

Soon the mood among them relaxes, and they're laughing.

'We're going to trip at Shell's place,' Manny is explaining to Jerry. 'Her old lady's at the beauty farm, and her old man's in Europe, so we like can have the place to ourselves cause Shell told the maids to split! And wait till you see her pad, man— outasite!'

Off Mesa now. Up. Along new elaborate houses invading the pristine desert. Houses a studied distance from each other in nervous luxury.

Now they're in the driveway of a sprawling white house. A brilliant glassed breezeway like a huge square diamond connects two sections of it. A rock and cactus garden courts the desert's natural beauty. In one garage there's a Cadillac like a haughty black animal; a Mercedes, sullen, aloof, is in another.

They enter the sprawling house.

Shell looks at it with contempt.

9

They pass large amber-glazed rooms expensively furnished, walls hung with paintings in gilded frames—a house like a cold museum in which each object is carefully assigned its studied, unyielding place. They cross the breezeway, glistening in the blue morning like an icicle, into another section of the house. This is Shell's apartment.

As if in reaction to the frozen props of the other rooms, the rooms here are deliberately, lovingly trashy, papered outrageously, intricate shapes and patterns zigzagging in and out of each other in loops, curves, circles. Carpets turn the floor into a sea of patched colors. Posters explode at odd angles. Cushions are tossed on the floor like dyed mushrooms. Even the walls of the kitchen—and there's a private kitchen in Shell's apartment —are covered with pop posters.

In a rectangle about the table in the kitchen, the four sit like an intense war council. There will be no preliminaries to taking the drug.

'We've got acid, mescaline, psilocybin,' Shell is announcing, as if tallying a treasure.

'Acid,' Cob chooses.

'Acid,' Manny echoes.

'Acid,' Jerry says.

'Okay—we'll all do the acid,' Shell says. She goes to the refrigerator and brings out a small sheet of paper.

'See, man, we'll all do the same shit, and then we can like be in on each other's trip,' Manny is explaining knowledgeably to

Jerry. 'Diggit, when people are tripping together—and they're righteous friends like us—you're all into the same trip. Like being in the same airplane—and like if it's smooth, everyone's grooving; and if it's bad, everyone bums.'

As intently as she separated the cocaine last night, Shell is cutting tiny squares from the sheet of paper; on it, very faintly, are just slightly gray smears, like dried raindrops. Careful not to touch the smears, she passes one of the tiny squares to Manny. Manny places the paper acid in his mouth, sucks on it, chews it. Cob does the same. Jerry imitates the others, sucking on the paper, then eating it. Shell takes hers.

Now in an extension of the recurring ritual of intimacy, they sip milk from the same glass, to settle their empty stomachs, the glass passing from mouth to mouth, like the joints of weed, the pipe of hashish: a surrogate touching of lips.

They move into the living-room. Shell lights some incense, its delicate perfumed smoke floating into the air.

Through a window leading to a small balcony, the barren desert is gold, the mountains magnificent in their aloof splendor.

Jerry waits tensely. He feels nothing, but it's too soon. Still, he's apprehensive. Will the acid let him down? Despite the sudden rush and the stoned numbness, even the cocaine disappointed him. It left him intact—and he craves total Escape, to be led away from the scarring initiation of death's totality; he craves the jarring of his world out of the quagmire of sorrow.

The stereo is on loudly. The sweet, harsh, tragic voice of Janis Joplin; a voice laughing and crying in the same note.

Minutes pass. A half hour. Shell begins to sway slightly to the music, as if it's passing gently through her. Slowly Cob joins her, but apart, sharing only sounds, as they did last night when they danced at The Seed. Now Manny is swaying too.

Determined to enter the current that is clearly propelling them, Jerry sits down with them. A profound disappointment. He still feels nothing. Nothing.

The stereo. Now the Rolling Stones. Mick Jagger. Sounds of willing rape.

'Fucking Jagger really fucking knows where the fucking shit's at!' Cob says admiringly.

'Right on,' Manny approves, raising a clenched fist.

'Oh, shit, man,' Cob derides good-humoredly, 'did you dig the Chicano dude telling me to right on?'

'And doing the power fist!' Shell laughs.

Cob joins her laughter.

Manny roars. He thrusts his fist higher: 'Power to the stoned people!'

'Right fucking on!' Cob approves.

'Fucking right-fucking-on!' Shell doubles over with laughter.

Still feeling nothing, Jerry watches them. Clearly, they're getting off on the drug. An incredible mellowing change is occurring in them; it's almost physical. The trace of anger, bitterness which stamped their faces earlier even when they smiled has faded. Now they smile innocently, with extravagant joy.

'Hey, where's that book with the pretty pictures, Shell?' Manny asks.

From a shelf filled with books, Shell brings out a large, expensive one of colorful, liquidy posters. Manny flips the pages, stops on one, staring at the melting colors. 'Oooo, oooo,' he coos, 'here come the pretty things!' His hand touches the page, and he laughs deliciously.

In fascination Jerry stares at Manny, then at the poster: a lush garden, arched walls leading past blazing flowers into clouds of tinted cotton. Beyond, in a deepening sky, dazzling stars.

Now Cob moves toward Manny and the picture. The two peer like conspirators at the page. A total transformation has occurred in Cob as he hovers over the page, his long hands moving playfully over the poster as if he were skipping through its world. Amazingly, he's a carefree child. Now Shell crawls to join them over the book, knitting an instant but still untouching closeness among the three. But Jerry is not a part of it.

'Diggit, Shell, right *here*!' Manny is pointing to the page, where arches lead past the garden into the universe. 'Zoom!' he says, as if plunging through its surface, his mind on a roller-coaster ride.

Shell flips the pages: '*This* is the one *I* dig!' she says, pointing to a poster depicting a man flying through a star-spangled path of sky.

'I diggit, I diggit!' Cob approves.

And so, suddenly, they're gentle children playing gentle-children's games; the astonishing transformation by the drug is complete. But Jerry has not been touched by it; the disappointment grates. He wants to be a part of their released, pristine happiness; he kneels on the floor with them, studying the posters.

Shell's eyes are liquid, staring at his face. She's more radiantly beautiful than ever, her eyes gleam like amber marbles.

Still nothing. Impatiently, Jerry moves away. From them and their happy world. Is he to be left out of it? He feels marooned in a sea of reality whose surface is death. Will he ever Escape then? He wanders into Shell's bedroom—away from the happy liberation of which he's not a part. He glances about the room. More posters. Elaborate prints of mythical kingdoms. Tacked to closet doors, cards with words—poems?—and line drawings printed on them. If he hadn't witnessed the Shell released by the acid, he would have wondered at the seeming incongruity of this room, the whole apartment. But it matches the gentle, awed child playing with Cob and Manny in the other room. He glances at the yellow bedcover on her bed. It's bordered with fragmented flowers, like burst stars.

Flowers. Burst stars.

Walls, striped colors, blue, red, yellow.

Walls. Striped colors. Blue. Red. Yellow.

Walls striped colors blue red yellow.

Wallsstripedcolorsblueredyellow.

Blue!   Yellow!   Red!

Yellowwwwwww . . . !

                                       RED!

             BLUE!

                 YELLOW!

BLUUUUUUUUUUUUUUE!

                                 RED!

        YELLOWWWWWWWW . . . !

Suddenly the deep-blue part of the stripes plunges back, the red dashes at him. Quickly the movement is reversed, red retreats, far, far back, the blue lunges. The yellow holds, quivering. In a moment the room is transformed as if every object in it—in the world!—has turned crystal, lit luminously by an inner light.

Suddenly Jerry *sees* the shape of the Stones' music coming from the other room. Sound invades the lunging colors, colors coat the flowing sound, sound melts on the colors into a visible symphony. Now they—sound, colors—contain him. No, he *is* the music, the music is profoundly him. And Shell's bed has become a yellow tide of waves breathing mysteriously. The room expands, outward, upward, into space, an expansion ruled by each beat of his heart.

And so he's been freed by the fantastic drug to enter a staggeringly beautiful world where colors and sound live!

Exploring that magnificent, outrageous world, he looks down at the fleecy rug on which he stands. It's a sea of motion, too—beautiful yet turbulent. Experimentally, he moves his feet over it; the fleece sighs. He sees each fiber tumbling down slowly in a whispering protest of motion.

Excitedly, he walks out of Shell's room, into the other. He isn't even dizzy. Floating, he's in perfect control in this new world ruled by spiraling visions. The room greets him like a live, glowing, crystal painting into which he's being allowed entry.

The three others still hover fascinated over the book of

posters. They seem enveloped in a fragile halo of yellow brightness.

Jerry laughs gloriously, laughs with the intense sense of discovery of the beauty—unseen till now—surrounding him. His lips open, to form what words? He doesn't know. Words which will shout the liberating discovery. The unexpected words finally erupt out of him: '*I love!*' he shouts.

Words without focus. I love . . .

'And *I* love!' Manny shouts exultantly.

'You love,' Shell conjugates the verb softly.

'They love,' Cob finishes the wayward conjugation in a sigh. Suddenly his hand moves out slowly before him as if to clear his vision. Instead he wipes away the solemn mood. He removes the dark sunglasses.

The movement of Cob's hand! For Jerry it had broken down into a million intricate maneuvers, the vast intricacy of a hand, moving! He had never seen it before. Nor any of this radiant world. Until now without the drug had he been totally blind? 'It's beautiful!' his own words come from a myriad directions.

'We're all beautiful!' Manny shouts. He stands. He raises his hands over his head as if to drape himself in the vibrations of joy, and he spins around.

'Yeah, we're *all* beautiful!' Cob joins him.

'Beautiful!' Shell's voice bursts.

Their words and his come at Jerry like colored winding forms. 'We're all beautiful!' he's repeating.

Cob's face! Peeling in layers of moods, it changes a dozen times before Jerry.

Knowing the drug's distortion of faces, 'What is my face doing?' Cob asks Jerry in amusement.

Jerry looks seriously at him. Cob's face changes swiftly from a long, angular, harsh, sinister face—and Jerry thinks, You look like death, and flees quickly from the thought—to that of a laughing, joyful child—to, finally, the face of an eager, desperate boy. Jerry nods at him, welcoming the latter.

'Look at *my* face!' Shell is giggling.

Jerry looks at her. A myriad transitions occur in a split instant, from hard, cold, brutal to peaceful, gentle, lovely. Stop there! Jerry feels the words, unspoken.

'What is my face doing?' the gentle face of Shell asks him delightedly.

Jerry merely laughs with the glory of discovery.

'What is it doing?' Shell insists laughingly.

Now Manny, Cob stand before Jerry, all giggling recklessly like children sharing a joke only they understand.

'Tell me!' Shell insists.

'No, man,' Jerry laughs. Shell's gentle face holds. 'It's beautiful,' he tells her.

'We're *all* beautiful!' Manny reminds them.

'And *now* what is it doing?' Shell continues. 'Is it changing?'

'Yeah!' Jerry says in amazement. 'It's . . . like it's peeling off and changing colors! And your eyelashes are fluttering like butterflies!'

'What's *mine* doing?' Manny asks delightedly.

Jerry studies Manny's face. Just the subtlest shaded distortion, as if a light is moving back and forth on him. 'Yours isn't doing too much,' Jerry confesses.

'That's because there's only one Manny, and many of us!' Cob laughs.

Manny makes extravagant monster faces, twisting his mouth, pulling his eyes. 'Now?'

Jerry roars with laughter. But suddenly, a moment that occurred without transition, he and Cob are looking steadily into each other's faces. Jerry sees again the anxious lost child.

Whether because he senses what Jerry is seeing in him or because of what he sees in Jerry's own tumbling face, Cob covers his face quickly with his hands.

'Look at me, look at me!' Manny shatters those strange moments. He's fashioned a ridiculous pointed cap, like a wizard's, from colored paper; and he's hopping about the room.

Shell shrieks with delight.

'Awoooooooooooooo000!'

'What's that?' Jerry asks apprehensively. A coiled spiral of sound without definite source surrounded him.

'That was just Manny howling.'

'That

                                       just

                        was

Manny

                     howling.'

Shell's voice tumbles into many throughout the room, like colored play blocks.

Suddenly Jerry is standing before a mirror staring at his own face. He focuses on his eyes. The boundaries of the mirror flee; his face, his eyes expand; they fill the world. He plunges past them. His body melts into pure being, lunging, he knows, into the universe, rushing toward the revelation of life's most beautiful, terrible secret . . . He turns away quickly, not yet ready to receive it.

He's facing the others: 'Is *my* face changing too?' he asks them earnestly.

Shell studies him seriously, her laughter stops abruptly. 'You look . . . like a sad angel,' she sighs.

'The fourth angel!' Manny reminds them gleefully.

'Yeah, man,' Cob says earnestly to Jerry, 'why are you so sad, man?'

'I'm not sad!' Jerry laughs at their momentary seriousness. 'Look! I'm laughing, man! Listen!' He roars with laughter. Yet when did it stop? Or did it? Is he still laughing? Then why is he aware of moisture in his eyes, on his cheeks? Tears? As if they merely formed on his face. Tears!

Cob turns swiftly away from him.

Then pulled from reality, the voice of Shell comes harsh, uncompromising, angered. 'Don't fucking cry!'

'I'm not crying, I'm laughing,' Jerry insists.

'Sure, the dude's like just laughing,' Manny says.

'Yeah—he's laughing so hard he's crying!' Shell welcomes happily.

Suddenly the mirth returns.

But Jerry turns silently from them. He moves, swims through the shifting sea of colors and sounds, Into Shell's room again. He's standing before one of the prints he ignored earlier. A shimmering Shangri-la. A golden palace surrounded by flower-lit trees, birds with rainbow plumages. A burst of sun. A streaming river. The water moves, the birds soar, and the sun . . .

The sun shatters in yellow blood on the river.

Yellow blood. Blood. And then like a physical object, the memory of his mother as she lay dying surfaces totally. Mother, his heart receives the memory. But the shining Shangri-la of the drawing—rendered powerfully magical by the drug—forces him, gradually, gently, to look beyond the pain. The yellow sun, the blue river. The river will carry the yellow blood to its primal origin, he thinks easily. Away from the thought of death, the drug has not only pulled him into the paradaisical whirlpool of the mythical kingdom of colors but it has expelled death.

Then, scenes—reality—shift, change without transition in abrupt flashes.

Flash! He's standing before Shell. 'I don't want it to end,' he hears himself say.

'It won't—for a while,' Shell assures him.

'I *never* want it to end!' Jerry repeats, fleeing—suddenly—crushed memories which now, in the magic-touched world of the drug, exist like ghosts.

'It's got to end,' Shell says slowly.

'No!' Jerry protests.

In the kitchen Shell peels an orange, she puts a section of it in each of their mouths. The *taste* of its beauty, its magnificent sweetness, enters Jerry's body sensually.

In the living-room, howling with laughter, Cob, Manny, Shell lie on the rugged floor, a three-pointed star. Jerry stares down at them. Suddenly he feels a sharp terror.

'Don't die,' his voice says urgently.

'Nobody's dying!' Shell says happily. She pulls at Manny and Cob. They whirl around in the formless dance of children.

Jerry wants to join them, but he can't. Why? His perceptions zoom backwards, inward, like a searchlight exploring him. He sees himself, alone, outside their circle, which he wants to join, but dare not.

They're outside. They're standing on the small balcony facing a vista of mountains and desert. Silently they stare at its iridescent splendor.

Jerry can see a single grain of sand separating from the others in that sea of sand; it gleams with its own identity. And, a sheet of paper in the wind—he sees its every twist, its every light movement in the breeze. A waltz of magnificent beauty. The outrageous, unbelievable splendor of this drugged world. Always there? Unseen till now? Hidden until the magic acid lifted away a heavy curtain of reality? Reality. This? Or the other? Can there be death in this world of vibrant colors and living beauty? And horror? And cruelty—can it exist here? The remembered savagery of yesterday with Stuart, the others trapped in the ugly dark house by them, stabs at his mind, but those memories are devoured by the shattering visual beauty surrounding him.

'Look, look!' Cob points to a bird.

They watch in awe. It soars magnificently within a visible breeze, which is blue like a satin ribbon.

They're standing in the desert, the balcony behind them.

Manny runs into the sand, throws himself on it, rolling in the myriad diamond grains like a freed young animal. The others join him, bathing deliriously in the sand.

Jerry looks intently at the sky. He's alone. The others are back in the house. How long has he been staring fascinated at the mysterious sheet of azure? A moment? A minute? An hour? The sky opens in blue shifting panels, like ice thawing gracefully on a blue lake.

Slowly he returns into the house.

He's standing in Shell's bedroom again, before the printed

86

cards tacked to a door: Colored line drawings, delicate, fine—
of trees, flowers; mystical Indian aphorisms.

He reads aloud from one. 'Even the severed branch grows
again . . .'

The infinite secret of life's cycle! The liberating discovery!
A branch, merely separated, but carrying a part of the whole
that produced it—one life flowing into another, erasing death!
He hears his voice full of joy—as if all pain—an enemy—has
withdrawn:

'I'm going to grow again!'

10

Suddenly for Jerry the magic retreats like a wave from the sea-
shore, and he's marooned again in reality, sorrow, death. *Even
the severed branch grows again!* He grasps desperately for the
words still floating on his mind, pulling them determinedly
from the drugged illumination, as if to retain them like an
anchor out of the magic; and the sea of the drugged world
rescues him powerfully once more, the magic returns in an
inundating wave; it carries him back to the living-room,
where:

The four stand in a rectangle looking at each other for
minutes; and each feels as if the others' world contains him, as
if his contains the others. And then they turn away, quickly
ending the crushing closeness.

'Let's go to the river!' Cob says.

'Shit, man, who can drive?' Manny reminds. 'We're too
ripped!'

'I can drive!'   'I can drive!'
                    'I can drive!'

But they know they can't.

'We'll hitchhike,' Shell offers.

'Outasite,' Manny agrees.

No further deliberation needed, they walk out of the house,
like silent pilgrims.

Outside, a magnificent breeze. Jerry smiles, raising his hand
to capture it.

Then the others raise their hands gently, to capture their own
share of the breeze.

'I caught it!' Manny announces in surprise.

88

'I caught it too,' Cob says, holding up his hand as if to exhibit the captured breeze.

'And *I've* got it too!' Shell exults.

'Me too!' Jerry says. He feels the breeze stirring restlessly in his hand. And then after moments of silence he says, 'Let's let it go—it's got to be free if it's a breeze.'

Slowly all four open their hands, releasing the captured breeze, which seems to glide to its flowing origin.

That moment, it wafted them with a touch of sorrow. Four figures on the street, outlined so small against the desert mountains, they stare into the vast sky after the lost, freed breeze.

The sky. A breathing presence. Jerry whispers to it the reverberating conjugation, I love, you love, we love.

Manny stands in the middle of the street, his hands stretched as far as they'll reach over his head, as if to grasp the sky. 'I want the sky to see me!' he announces joyfully.

'Me too!'   'Me too!'   'Me too!'

They all stand in the middle of the street, their bodies stretching toward the sky.

Now they're walking toward the highway, down the hill. The street curls, shortens before them, now it stretches, lengthens. For blocks they walk along a beautiful, warmly frozen eternity.

Then they stumble on a jagged, patched shadow. They peer at it with profound interest. Separated curiously from its origin —and they do not search for it—the shadow spills sinisterly.

'Is it pretty or ugly?' Jerry asks.

'Ugly,' Cob decides.

They abandon it quickly.

'I'm hungry,' Manny says, spotting a supermarket nearby. Within the drug's overwhelming clarity, the store looks improvised, fashioned out of flimsy colored blocks.

Without pondering the decision, they walk into the supermarket, exploring the aisles. The store tilts, heavy with cardboard colors. Before the dairy products, Jerry reaches easily for a container of sour cream. Opening it, he scoops it out with his hand, eating it happily, now offering it eagerly to the others, who scoop the cream with their fingers. Cob goes to the meat counter, opens a package of cold cuts, generously passes pieces to them, and they eat happily, responding naturally and without inhibition to the need of their hunger.

Now Manny is holding a can of whipped cream. He's explaining: 'The first hit is like laughing gas, man—but it's got to be the *right* brand of whipped cream. Then you hold this end to your nose, press the little dude, and hit; it gives you an outasite rush.' He inhales the gas, begins to laugh. 'Pow!' he indicates it hit his head. Now he holds the can to Jerry, who imitates the motions. But only whipped cream gushes out, coating his nose like cotton candy.

A woman in grotesque curls stares at them aghast. Enraged, despising their innocent freedom of these moments, she holds her shopping cart like a weapon ready to run them down.

'Want some?' Jerry earnestly offers her the sour cream.

The woman turns fiercely from them, driving the cart like a tank. But in those moments, Jerry saw her mean face crumbling before him, folding over into a hideous, tortured rubber mask, melting. The curlers transformed into rolled horns pasted on her head, her pores opening ferociously, she had become a violent, irrational—yet strangely frightened—animal.

As they walk unperturbed out of the store, Manny says, 'Thank you,' to one of the checkers.

Casually holding out their thumbs for a ride, they walk along the highway.

A ride. A youngman. 'Where are you going?'

'To the river,' Shell answers.

To the river. Jerry feels himself flowing. The river. The revelation of the stunning secret! The river in the paradaisical drawing in Shell's bedroom—he remembers it. Blood on the river: blood, river, sea. Ocean . . .

They get into the car.

Jerry catches an image of his own face trapped in the rear-view mirror. A violent stranger suddenly! His eyes look sinister to him. They must have looked like that to Stuart out of the darkness. Turn away! To: a cactus by the road, it grasps his attention totally even as the car speeds by it. The plant stands erectly young, sighs, folds over, old, crumbles. Dies. Dies . . . His mother had resisted death, and he had sought to pull her away from it by clinging to her hand and pushing his breath into her. The severed branch! he grasps. But his mind pulls. At the point of inevitable surrender to the tide carrying her away—*where?!*—what did she think? Again he grabs the anchor from the magic world. Even the severed branch grows again! And blood and the river flow . . .

'I'm going in the opposite direction,' the driver of the car is saying, and they're getting out.

The opposite direction. Jerry frowns, feeling a great heaviness. No! I want to flow with the river, he thinks.

Again casual thumbs. Another ride. A jovial middle-aged man. He sighs wistfully as if to himself: 'I wish I was as free as you.'

'Sometimes we're not free,' Jerry hears his pensive words, and he remembers last night—a blackness, that's all.

'We're always free,' Cob asserts.

'Free!' Manny's arms attempt to imitate a bird's wings.

'As free . . .' Shell says slowly, '. . . as free as the breeze we captured.'

At the crossroads, the man lets them off.

'What are you doing, Jerry?' Shell is roaring with laughter.

'Hugging this tree!' Jerry answers, his arms embrace an enormous, green-leafed tree.

'Let me! Let me!' Cob hugs the tree tightly too. Jerry's, Cob's hands link in a circle about the tree.

'Me, too!' Manny joins them eagerly—and then Shell.

All four hug the tree tightly. Then slowly they drift away from the tree and each other.

A van picks them up immediately.

Now, the river. The Rio Grande. The four get out of the van.

The river!

Jerry stands looking at it. It courses like a wild young animal—dark, vibrant water flows freely. Jerry holds his breath in wonder.

Along the levee, bands of stray young people, barefoot, long-haired, semi-nude, camp in tribal clusters. Some wear beads like pretty badges on brown exposed bodies. Headbands contain flowing hair. The new Indians. Several hundred young color-splashed, sun-loved exiles fleeing the gray straight world. Some naked youngmen and girls swim unselfconsciously in the river. Wine bottles passing communally from mouth to mouth gleam purple, green, like precious jewels capturing the sun's rays. The pervasive odor of smoked grass wafts the country air delicately. The mellow sound of guitars holds its own against the rock sounds from radios, tapes in cars—some cars new and expensive, some studiedly old, decorated with flowers and splashed colors, all parked at odd angles as if abandoned within the happy carnival atmosphere of the levee. Pastel laughter joins soaring frisbees like colored moons slicing the air. A lingering beauty exists on the banks of the river.

But Jerry's eyes will not yet budge from the mysterious alive water.

Manny is taking crazy giant steps along the bank, studying the imprint of each foot. Each time he places his foot down, he creates a fascinating hollow, quickly filled, the sand trembling into complex, strange shapes. Stilled motion! He turns to the others, smiles, certain they, too, sharing the drug, share the mysterious worlds his footprints are uncovering.

Now—is it possible in the clear afternoon?—did time merely hop from here to there?—a vagrant cloud has crossed the sky, shedding tiny drops of rain. The sun still shines around it. For seconds it rains sun and water. The four feel the rain as they never felt it before and they rub it into their bodies. Then the shower ended, merely enough moisture to set the ground steaming in sighs, barely visible ghosts.

Long hair flowing like a dark Messiah's, Cob swaggers

alongside the river. His smiling face tilts, welcoming the moist heat.

Jerry wrests his look from the river.

And the four idle along the levee, stopping occasionally to gaze at a vagrant river flower sputtering like a dyed flame, or at long, long blades of wild grass which reach their knees along lush patches adjoining the water. The four study each object raptly, sharing its shape, its scent, its color.

Here and there, familiar faces call out to them, they pause, nod, smile, move on to another cluster of often-stoned smiles. Somebody lights a number, passes it to them, but, now, they reject it. It may bring them down from the acid peak.

The trees. On the opposite side, on the bank across the river, they grow thickly, a tangle of green like a misplaced forest lost in the miles of desert beyond. Delicate lace fans of leaves whisper, seem to move close to Jerry from across the fantastic river. But his eyes compulsively shift slightly away to a strait scorched by a recent fire. And the trees there are smoke-blackened and desolate. Suddenly to Jerry they're the props of a sinister, forbidden country. Death could crouch there in ambush, fleeing the drug's powerful expulsive magic. Quickly he seeks out the river. And the anxiety withers. The river! It stretches to infinity. Infinity, a gentle, flowing river.

A red frisbee sighs weightlessly over them. They all look in unison, holding their breaths at the beauty of its slow weightless motion. They nod silently: Yes!

Then again: flashes!

A stark, incongruous woman, much older than the others here, is marching from a car defiantly like a hostile general invading peaceful territory. In giant strides, she leads a dog by a leash. She wears goggled glasses; flaming auburn hair is piled on her head like a barbarous trophy . . . All four turn quickly away from her.

Stamping hooves! Two magnificent horses, mounted by two youngmen. Jerry rushes toward the animals, they bolt. 'I just want to touch you,' Jerry explains wistfully. He remembers the brown cat's unyielding yellow eyes.

A young girl huddles along the bank on the grass. She trembles fitfully, obviously seized by a raiding inner fear. Her eyes are glazed as she turns about her in terror as if assaulted invisibly.

'Bum tripping,' Cob says.

But how could the beautiful world of the drug ever turn against anyone? Jerry wonders, staring at the girl. Never against him! He's approached the terrified girl, to comfort her. But the girl recoils from him, rushing away insanely.

Suddenly all four are riding on the hood of a car along the bumpy dirt road. Others along the levee applaud and shout in happy approval. Manny howls like a cowboy riding a young mustang—'Yahoooo!' Cob waves at the young people like a popular potentate. Shell smiles, her hands extended as if to include everyone in her greeting. Jerry is aware of joy like a warm companion.

A strange youngman completely naked stumbles along the river as if through a foreign terrifying country, his eyes unfocused, wide. Jerry frowns. But this time he will not approach him as he did the similarly stunned girl.

They're lying on the tall, tall grass, together, barefooted— Cob, Jerry, Manny shirtless.

On a small island of sand on the narrow river, an island which extends over the water like a distorted parabola, two shirtless youngmen crouch over the sand, also drug-tripping.

The four stand over the two in fascination.

One of the two holds out a handful of sand to Shell. A treasure of a million dazzling diamonds, golden needles! Taking it, she allows the sand to seep through her hands. Jerry catches the filtered particles in his. Their hands touch barely as the sand filters from the one into the other.

'Can we play too?' Shell asks the two youngmen crouched on the moist sand.

Both smile, nodding, welcoming them.

The four sit down, burying their fingers into the precious moisture. Each fistful of sand is a design of intricate geometric beauty, silver, gold, white, yellow.

They sit in a circle, the six. And as if to a silent signal issued by the drug, a silent agreement, they begin to construct an elaborate castle of sand. Occasionally they will look in wonder at each other, smile, go on. Now the intricate castle, with tunnels, turrets, towers, moats is finished. They study it in amazement, trying to grasp its dazzling beauty.

Suddenly Cob stands up, viewing the castle fiercely. The magic of the drug retreats rudely. He's aware of the frailty of the complex castle they've constructed. The rising river will destroy what he helped to build. No! Savagely he stamps on the castle with his feet, grinding it down, annihilating it.

'What are you doing?' Shell shouts at him.

The others echo her protest.

Manny confronts Cob. 'You fucking tore down our castle, why did you fucking tear it down?'

'Because it's shit!' Cob says, he stands apart. The drug has abandoned him totally on a wave of darkness pulling him viciously out of the magic country. He puts on the dark sunglasses, his face is somber again, a dark, brooding mask. He feels a current of anger charging through him. And what is its object? Who?

The others are looking down at the debris of the sand castle.

Shell studies the crushed castle. Her face darkens. With a muffled shout, she passes her foot violently over what remains of it. 'Yeah,' she says, 'it's all shit.'

Then with his hands—fists—Manny too begins to pound on the castle. 'Shit!' he echoes Cob, Shell. Anger infectious in the delicate drugged stage, the two other youngmen join them, stamping on the sand. 'Shit, shit, shit!'

And then Jerry lunges toward the group—at first as if to stop them, but, now, instead, to join the destruction. His bare feet beat on the crushed sand, obliterating the castle totally: 'Shit, shit, shit!' he says fiercely.

The river courses in diamond rivulets created by the sun.

Wherever it has lodged in their bodies, their minds, the drug is running its course. The artificial beauty is diminishing quickly.

Suddenly, reality in violent gusts!

For Jerry—and when did he suddenly search it again?—the river no longer stretches endlessly to eternity. It too ends. Just ends.

The others remain staring down at the crushed castle.

II

Silently the four walk away from the two they joined.

The afternoon sun floats in the clear sky.

'It's ending,' Jerry says, in order not to say 'It's ended.' A surrender from the dazzling drugged world. 'Let's do some more dope!' he says anxiously. He doesn't yet want to commit himself to viewing reality, afraid it may be unchanged, the pain still sharply there, the presence of death a brutal knife in his mind.

'Yeah!' Manny approves.

'Later, tonight,' Shell offers.

'Night-tripping!' Manny is enthusiastic.

A black silence drapes Cob.

On a strip of tall grass ahead, two girls sit, legs crossed in the lotus position, staring at the water, beyond.

'They're meditators,' Shell realizes.

'Are those the weird freaks that don't do dope?' Manny asks, shaking his head.

As if affronted by their ostensible serenity, Cob swaggers up to them. The smile is incongruous on his clouded face. He asks the girls sharply, 'You want some dynamite dope?'

Jerry notices a small bundle beside the two: a baby.

The two girls stir as if to adjust to the sharp intrusion. 'We don't do dope any more,' one of them says; she's dark, straight-haired, starkly plain.

'Then what are you doing here with all the dopers?' Shell asks them.

'We came to the city for supplies—we're in a commune,'

says the other, an intense, blond girl. 'We wanted to meditate by the river.'

The river. Perhaps like him to confront a vast mystery in it. Jerry smiles at the girls.

Perhaps sensing a lurking tenderness in him, and hostility from Shell and Cob, the dark girl addresses Jerry: 'You ought to come to our commune, it's peaceful.'

Peace. The word embraces Jerry.

Shell reacts quickly: 'He's the fourth angel—we're the angels—and he wouldn't dig a straight commune.'

The baby begins to whimper like a chirping bird.

'Whose is it?' Shell asks the girls.

'Mine,' the blond girl says, holding it in her arms.

'Shouldn't you have him at home, where you can fucking take care of him?' Cob asks angrily. 'With his father?'

'Wherever he's loved, that's where he's all right,' says the blond girl, sheltering the child from Cob's fierce face.

Cob shakes his head in angry disapproval.

The child in her fleeing totally, Shell attacks brutally: 'Were you meditating when the baby happened? Or were you stoned?' The bitter turn of her lips, a bitterness erased during the hours of the acid trip, is there again, a brand on the beautiful face.

'Oooo-eee,' Manny squirms.

The blond girl's eyes blaze. She breathes deeply.

'You're really weird chicks,' Cob says.

You really are, Jerry wants to echo. Beyond his control he feels a sharp need to strengthen the recurrent meanness, as he did yesterday, even if it was largely as a witness to another's terror. Still, he was not able now to echo Cob's accusation of the girls. The drug's barely lingering mellowness? He still doesn't dare to test the illuminations of the drug within the real world: more afraid now—because there was that sputtering to join the anger. He merely turns from the girls.

The four walk away.

There's a growing festiveness along the levee as the afternoon deepens. Someone has fashioned a swing from a tree, and a young girl soars through the air like a colorfully plumed bird. A group by a star-and-flower-decorated van plays a harmonica, a guitar, soft drums. Apple wine and a pipe filled with grass, shared openly, link them together.

A bearded youngman's voice rises, full, in a song:

> 'The sheep's in the meadow,
> The cow's in the corn,
> Now is the time for a child to be born . . .'

The four stop. Listen.

> 'He'll cry for the moon,
> And he'll laugh at the sun,
> If he's a boy he'll carry a gun . . .'

Cob's head is cocked quizzically.

> 'If it should be that our baby's a girl,
> Never you mind if her hair doesn't curl.
> Rings on her fingers and bells on her toes,
> And a bomber above her wherever she goes . . .'

Moodily the four walk away.

Barefoot, a staff in his hand, hair a wiry reddish tangle, an intense youngman, almost emaciated, wearing only a loin-cloth, walks into the weekend throng. At first his voice was a mumble, and then it rose into a loud, vibrating exhortation: 'Turn to Jesus!' he shouts. 'Only the Lord Jesus Christ can help you! Drugs are not the answer! Turn to Jesus!'

'A Jesus freak,' Cob derides.

'Jesus loves us!' the prophet-like youngman shouts along the river.

Suddenly Jerry remembers the church they were in yesterday, his anger at the presence within it—the crucified figure the victim of that presence; like his mother. He withdraws urgently from his thoughts, he echoes the magic words that saved him earlier, the anchor retrieved from the drugged revelations. Even the severed branch grows again! Did it work? Has he expelled death? He withholds the crucial verdict—he focuses on the river.

'Jesus loves us!' the emaciated youngman repeats.

'No one loves us!' Shell yells suddenly at him.

'You're wrong! You're wrong!' the intense youngman pleads with her. 'He died to save us—and I know, because like him I was crucified. On smack!' He thrusts out his arms like the crucified Jesus. Needle marks slash them as if a knife had slit them. 'One true Jesus! The power of the cross! I saw his face, I heard his voice, and he touched and sealed my arms forever from the needles. And I'm saved because he loves me! Jesus loves us! We're saved in his love!'

'No one loves anyone!' Shell shouts at him. She begins to walk after him, as if to stalk him.

'Just us!' Manny says urgently. 'We love each other,' he calls to her.

'Jesus loves us!' the emaciated youngman persists passionately, and his body is quivering as if about to lose control. Suddenly he stops walking, he turns sharply. He faces Shell.

Both open their lips, to speak—in anger?—in despair? But no words form.

Shell seems suddenly spent.

The others have walked to join her.

The intense youngman whispers uncertainly: 'He does love us, he really does . . .'

Shell shakes her head, slowly.

The eyes of the youngman glisten.

At that moment Jerry's hand moved impulsively out toward him. He withdraws it quickly, harshly.

Shell turns away. 'Let's split,' she says abruptly.

They walk along the levee. On the road they got a ride quickly in a van suffused in the odor of shared grass.

Minutes later: inside Shell's apartment. They're in the same room where this morning's magic trip began. Jerry feels a sudden sorrow. Objects no longer glow like lighted crystals. Is everything, then, unchanged? Inside himself? But he knows the commitment to that answer must be postponed for now. Allowing tonight's drug to work more magic. And tomorrow . . . Tomorrow, alone, inside the house where he lived with his mother; inside the graveyard of memories; tomorrow . . . Then the drug's permanent power will be tested: the illuminations rendered real or illusory. For now, with the others—and he'll call his sister to feed the cats tonight, he can't yet face the test— he can postpone the thoughts that will test his liberation from the clutch of death's presence.

Shell and Cob are in the kitchen. Jerry stares after them. He feels an intense compulsiveness to discover . . . 'What's between them?' his words came casually aimed at Manny.

'Huh, man?' Manny is bewildered.

'Between Shell and Cob, what?' Jerry commits himself further.

'Oh, shit, man, you know, like we're the four fucking angels,' Manny says.

'But what's it all about—with all of us?' Jerry hears words. Has the faded drug led him onto this plateau?

Manny frowns, as if he's concentrating very deeply in order to remember Shell's words. 'It's to find out—uh—to . . . Like being strong, man. Uh, experience, you know; an experience trip. Like where the shit is—uh—so that . . . To find out . . .'

'To find out what?' Jerry questions.

'I don't know,' Manny shrugs. Again he frowns. 'Hey! Maybe Shell's trying to get into *our* freak heads!' He laughs to erase the seriousness.

'Maybe we'll get into her head first,' Jerry's words come intensely.

'Shell's head?' Manny laughs. 'Man, it's not her *head* I want to get into.'

And so, no, Manny has not made it with Shell, Jerry knows. And Cob?—has he?

In the kitchen all four eat hungrily, cold roast, cheese, fresh fruit. But caught in the threatening hollow of unbudging time, they're aware of a strident tension.

Finished eating, Jerry moves away from it—especially from the acute sense of Cob's hostility. He walks again into Shell's bedroom. Now it's merely a colorful room, the print of the lush paradise through which he wandered earlier led by the drug is merely a print. He approaches the cards tacked to the closet doors. He reads again, 'Even the severed branch grows again.' His not yet fully tested anchor . . . He shifts his thoughts. Strange that Shell should have tacked that aphorism here. What does it mean to her? The severed branch. . . . From what does she feel severed? He feels close to the part of Shell—the beautiful enigma—represented by these cards, the prints of unreal kingdoms.

He returns to the living-room, joining the others on the floor. A four-pointed star, they sprawl on the floor. They don't touch. The entrapping silence seals them as the afternoon wanes into evening. Yellow light still floods the desert, shadows deepen, the mountains are dark. The southwest sun seems determined to linger lazily into the night.

Tears. The word shaped on Jerry's mind. No, not shaped, it was as if it merely descended on him. From where? Tears. He tries to imagine Shell crying. He stares at her. Cry, Shell! he thinks deliberately, demanding that his imagination supply tears coming from her eyes. But the image refuses to form. He tries harder. *Cry, Shell!* Still, the image will not shape.

The sun has disappeared reluctantly, spilling its twilight glow on the desert like embers. Gray darkness filters the room. The taped music—Janis Joplin again. Janis of the laughing, sobbing voice.

Dead.

Jerry thinks: Janis Joplin is dead. But he cannot think 'My mother is . . .' The word won't form, he won't surrender. He forces his attention on Joplin's voice. A voice stilled by death. Memories beyond control. His mother's funeral, the box prepared for the waiting grave, the abundant flowers, the crucifix over it, the priest took the crucifix and handed it to him . . . Is the unbearable pain still there? Has the drug left it intact? *Even the severed branch grows again*—those words are becoming an incantation. Again he backs away from his thoughts. Tomorrow—in the stilled house—he'll face it all.

The desert is veiled in gray twilight. The spilled sun yields slowly to the gathering darkness. Like a cloud, night floats over the mountains.

Then Shell gets up, severing the four-pointed star. She leaves the room. Returns. With pills. Slick, red. One glass of water for the shared communion. Cob takes a pill, then Manny; now Shell. Jerry looks at the capsule. 'It's not acid,' he says in disappointment.

'It's just as good,' Shell assures him.

'It's mescaline,' Cob says.

'Will it do the same?' Jerry asks.

'Yes,' Shell promises; 'maybe better.'

The night trip.

Shell turns on lights about the apartment, suffusing it in color to welcome the blaze of the magic.

Liquid minutes pass.

Then: 'Here come the pretty things again!' Manny announces happily. 'Oooo-eee!' he greets them.

Then Jerry saw the smile blessing Shell's face like the reflection of a halo. She sways her head slowly, her hair tumbles over her forehead; her face is radiant with magic, the magic of the other Shell.

Getting off too, Cob bends his head and begins to laugh softly. Then Manny catches the laughter—and then Shell. The transformation again!

And then Jerry felt it like a powerful wave, a vast rush of colors which swept him. A powerful vortex! The beautiful world flashing! A burst kaleidoscope! Shapes melt, form figures, blend, re-form, advance. The room widens, stretches, no longer contained within the confines of its physical dimensions, a part of the eternity of space.

'Yes!' Jerry welcomes that world again. And then he too begins to laugh gloriously, joining the others—all on the floor, laughing happily.

Then, as if closeness is unbearable, he stands up suddenly. A part of him still not touched by the drug pulls away, guarding his isolation, the closed world of himself and his mother . . . And looking down at the three, he sees three fallen angels. And I'm the fourth, he thinks. And remembers the slain dragon crushed by the angel—or was the angel crushed by the dragon? Quickly thoughts without shape come profoundly to him, are eroded by others. 'Just us,' he says aloud, grasping the end of one thought, which already evaporated.

'Just us,' Cob echoes slowly. Abruptly, he stands before Jerry. Again they stare at the respective vicissitude of their changing faces. Jerry waits for the one face of Cob's that he will greet. It emerges—the face of a yearning child.

Slowly Cob raises his hand as if actually to touch Jerry's face, an assertion of this morning's vague gesture.

'Diggit,' Manny says, 'Cob actually wants to stop Jerry's face from changing!'

Assaulted by the words, Cob drops his hand. He sits down quietly.

Laughter stops, drowned in silence.

Jerry's world, beyond control. His mother's body surrounded by flowers. He knelt before her, kissing her, touching her face; the makeup was glued to his fingers . . . But! Within the drugged world he can banish death at will with: flashing colors! vibrating sounds! He commands them to seize his attention. And they do.

Now all four are sitting on the floor before a box of beads, stones—rocks broken open revealing miniature crystal caverns like tiny unexplored kingdoms. The gleaming treasure is spread before them on a rug. They peer at the molten spectrum of colors. Eagerly they *touch* the colors.

Manny is staring raptly at a fistful of beads, which squirm, breathe, dance. Cob reaches for one shiny object after another, as if to find the perfect one. Simultaneously Shell and Jerry choose a long, long strand of beads. Held mutually, the strand unites them like a colored, delicate chain.

Then Manny too is holding the strand. And then Cob. All four bound by the colorful necklace, they sit looking at it and at each other.

Yet for a moment, an intruding reality shot through the magic, and to Jerry they seemed suddenly: four angels declaring war.

Shell and Manny drift away. Cob and Jerry remain on the floor facing each other, holding the strange chain of beads. Then they abandon it on the floor. And stand.

Suddenly Manny is playing with a ball—like a multi-colored orange. Segments of red, yellow, blue, purple. Tossed into the air, the ball is a suspended flashing sun. It floats very slowly, like a balloon—to the floor. And rises, gathering its clash of beautiful colors. Tenderly Manny throws it to Shell; and equally tenderly, she throws it to Jerry. Jerry holds it momentarily. Then instead of throwing it, he brings it to Cob like a present. Abruptly, Cob drops the ball. It bounces. Rises into the air. Falls.

Falls! Manny's world. The dropped ball! He felt as if his body collapsed with it, evaporated. And all that remains is a confused, suddenly terrified mind. Terror mounts in an instant, like spreading fire. His vision narrows into a long distortion of darkening colors. He closes his eyes, afraid, lost suddenly in a strange world. The fear is over—a moment like a year's nightmare blackness.

Now, as if it were in command, the music seizes their attention; notes which only now can they hear buried within the familiar rhythms.

'Let's go for a walk,' Cob suggests.

Manny's world. The fear brushes him like a dark wing. 'I'm too fucking ripped, I'd get lost,' he says. He tries to laugh.

'We'll take care of you,' Jerry says. He senses Manny's confusion. This time, beyond the colors and changing faces, the hallucinations, Jerry is aware of a heavy intensity exposing subtle vibrations: Emotions almost physical, naked. Like witnessing a play within a box: reality framed for careful observation. It was so that Jerry—and he remembered the terrified dazed girl, the lost naked youngman by the river earlier—it was so that he felt Manny's fear.

Recovered, Manny says quickly: 'Hell, I'm up for a walk, let's go!'

Outside.

They pause before surrendering to the desert night.

Manny remains close to Jerry.

Jerry's world. His soul fuses with the breathing night, the sighing stars, and it soars freely through the universe.

They stare at the darkly luminous sky.

So beautiful, Jerry thinks. The word assumes a shape, floats about him, blesses him. Beautiful. He sees the night in swirling spirals through the sky. The sky. The river. A secret. An answer.

A breeze kisses Shell's hair, raises it slowly, then drops it lightly.

12

They trudge on, like explorers through a new country. Totally theirs. And Jerry is aware of a magnificent unity and continuity within the drug's unraveling universe. Sensed during the acid trip, the awareness now engulfs him. As if ordered gently by a benign mellowing sky, flowers, alert, grow before his eyes; trees, rustling softly, bend, then rise erectly; cactuses breathe and pulse with life, rest, bloom again in bursts of color. All, illumined by the night's silver, is involved in a cycle of life, death, rebirth, resurrection.

Resurrection!

Jerry captures the word as he did the image of the severed branch to retain it when the drug fades, a guarded piece of its magic. Resurrection and the severed branch! He orders his mind to 'see' his mother: the beautiful green eyes, the fair complexion, the gentle, glorious, warm smile. Yes! He knows the drug's illuminations will lead him away from the black abyss.

Manny's world. Fear. 'Do you know where we fucking are, man?' he asks.

'Yes,' Cob says with determined certainty.

'Sure,' Shell underscores.

Aware sharply of Manny's new apprehension, Jerry hears a rudely intruding sound he knows did not occur: *Whooosh!* The mysteries of the universe, stirring, exposed by the drug, he tells himself. 'It's beautiful!' But this time he used the words, frantically uttered, to pull him away from . . . Manny's powerfully projected fear: unexpectedly it assaulted the beautifully ordered universe.

Manny's world. They're traveling through a confused, tangled country.

Jerry waits for Manny. Shell and Cob march ahead.

'It's okay, man,' Jerry tells Manny. Despite the earlier stunning revelation, and he clutches it in his mind, Jerry is aware of a subtle difference in tonight's drugged trip. Perhaps it's the night—and within it Manny's conveyed fear—that accounts for a barely glimpsed hint of apprehension. But recurrently the flashing hallucinatory beauty and the illuminations within it conquer it.

'Yeah, man? It's okay? Yeah?' Manny says. His face is drained. The strange fear recedes, further, further. To show himself, and Jerry, that he's all right, he begins to giggle. But is the terror stalking him, retreating only to gain momentum for a massive assault? He laughs louder.

Now the drug has destroyed time—it occurs in islands within space.

Suddenly! They're on the highway. It had reached them. They're hitchhiking. Metallic elongated shapes of cars pass by like chrome ribbons, their lights long strips of colored, luminous wax.

A car stops. Voices swirl about them. The faces of two youngmen shift, strip in layers. More time melts.

Suddenly! 'Here's where we get off.' Shell's voice as if within a bottle.

Suddenly! They're on the concrete island between lanes on the Mesa highway. Lights float within the velvety night. Manny takes a step off the curb, reaching out swiftly with his hand toward a car gliding by eerily.

'Watch it, man!' Shell calls.

'What are you doing?' Cob laughs.

Manny says seriously, 'I want to touch the lights. I want to know are they warm or cold.' The matter is of infinite importance.

'They're whatever you want them to be,' Shell says. 'It's your trip, your world.' And her world—she feels total.

108

Night travelers, they cross the street.

Cob's world. His mother! And, Janet!—the feline face he ignored this morning burns on his mind. If he could get lost forever in the ordered anarchy.

They're in the residential area of Kern Place, heavily treed, with angled streets.

Ripped by the weeks-long wind just ended, a long branch dangles weirdly, projecting a strange shadow on the street. Cob crouches forlornly over it. The others study it with him. This time Jerry pronounces the verdict: 'It's ugly.' They retreat quickly from the dead shadow.

Familiar houses have been transformed into distorted drawings out of children's storybooks: some sinister—they turn away from them—some funny—all four laugh in unison.

Before them a children's playground is outlined gray like a giant erector set. They approach it. Madeline Park, a small, two-block park. Quickly Cob climbs a concrete whale with a slide on its side. Gleefully, breaking the mood the strange shadow put them into, he slides down. Manny does it too. 'Wheeeeee!' And then Jerry, laughing happily.

Shell sits on a swing, pushing it slowly with her toes. The swing gains steady momentum. Now she pushes faster. Faster. Suddenly she's flying through space. The beauty of outrageous motion envelops her. Almost touching the ground, she leans back—a dark soaring bird in the night. She pushes the swing faster . . . Shell's world: cleansed! Purified by motion! Wind!

Then Cob is behind her, laughing, pushing at the swing and laughing. It soars as if to join the starry heaven of Texas sky. Shell laughs, too. The more she laughs the harder Cob, laughing too, pushes.

Manny and Jerry study them.

Suddenly Jerry sees again—appearing in a flash—the demonic-child's face of Cob; and although he's still laughing as he pushes Shell on the swing, there's a sudden fury in the movements.

A desperate pendulum about to lose control, the swing reaches higher and higher. Still, Shell laughs. Cob pushes with greater force, ferocity. Yet both are laughing.

Anxiety growing, 'You're gonna freak her out, man!' Manny shouts at Cob.

'Freak who out?' The words form about Shell, rush from the swing. 'Freak who out?' And she laughs.

Cob pushes still harder. 'Give up?' he asks her.

'I *never* give up!' her voice is hurled from the swing.

Cob pushes harder, faster. 'Give up?'

'No!' Shell's voice comes. 'Push as hard as you can, man! Harder! Faster!'

The swing veers toward loss of control.

Still, Shell is laughing, but all mirth has left her laughter. And Cob's is drained too, the skeleton of laughter, its depleted sounds only.

Jerry *feels* Shell's terror. Shell's? Or is it Cob's? Or only his own? Shell's . . . *Can* Shell feel terror? *Cry, Shell!*

But Shell is laughing. 'Faster!' she yells.

His face dark—no longer smiling—Cob pushes the swing savagely as if to tear it from its props. 'You give up?'

'No!'

A focus for his recurring fear. 'Give up, Shell, give up!' Manny shouts with genuine terror.

'*No!*' Shell yells.

Suddenly, his body quivering, Cob feels dizzy. Abruptly he abandons the swing, which keeps soaring, but slower each time, its arc narrowing. And then it stops. Shell remains sitting on it triumphantly. She faces Cob. '*You* gave up,' she says.

He stares at her. A darkness beyond the night's shades his face.

Then, as if a cord of tension has been disconnected, they all laugh gaily, simultaneously, children again.

The darkened park.

Abandoned on the path is a child's toy, a colored plastic ball-like rattle attached to a stick. Manny picks it up, shakes it experimentally. Wondrous sounds. He rattles it again. Then he rushes at the others playfully with it.

They see him running toward them in slow motion.

Jerry turns from the stick. Suddenly sinister, it looks like a severed head on a pike.

Manny hands the stick to Shell; an offering.

'It's beautiful,' she acknowledges.

'Let me see it,' Cob takes it from her. 'Yeah,' he agrees, and he hands it gravely to Jerry for his examination.

But Jerry backs away from it. He heard his voice, 'It's dead.' His world, a peculiar focus, a stark framing of the immediate scene. A disorienting moment, an island of insanity; they were insane children in a twisted world. The disorientation melts. Exposed only fleetingly, the subterranean depths beneath the drug's beauty had been stirred.

Shell rattles the stick. 'No, man, it's not dead, it's *alive*!' she says firmly.

'Like us!' Manny exults, touching his body.

The sound of trees, of grass; they perceive it—the rhythmic pulse of the universe, of its props, Jerry knows.

They move slowly, Manny holding the toy-stick which Jerry rejected. Manny raises it, shaking it occasionally as if to ward off the lurking shadows.

They wander in and out of streets, alleys, past hovering houses, observing a particular one as it angles curiously.

'I'm afraid,' Manny whispers uncontrollably.

Jerry looks at Manny's face. Again, swiftly all color drained from it. Yes, it's like the terrified face of the girl by the river, the naked youngman. *Whoosh!* Jerry hears the strange sound-less sound again intruding recurrently, with Manny's fear, on the beautiful world.

'No, you're not afraid!' Shell insists, facing Manny.

'I mean, I just . . . Like where does my mother live?' Manny asks vaguely. The drug is invading reality.

'You want to go home?' Cob accuses.

'You don't need her,' Shell says firmly to Manny. 'You don't need anyone, just us.'

'I don't want to go home,' Manny says uncertainly, as if to convince himself.

Jerry's world, memories. He sat forlornly outside the funeral home until the sun came out . . . The severed branch, resurrection! he repeats to himself the incantation.

'Let's hitchhike to the old house by the bar,' Cob offers.

'No!' Jerry rejects quickly. There's a pall of ugliness over the memory of last night's adventures.

'Stuart . . .' Manny begins vaguely. Then he giggles, 'Those two dam dudes, man—they were *screwing*, man!'

'Yeah,' Cob's voice is cold, out of yesterday's real world

'We'll go to the river,' Shell offers easily.

'Yeah!'   'Yeah!'   'Right on!'

They thumb on the highway. And now the drug's mellowness has spread, coating the night in soft, dark velvet. A car stops, drives them to the crossroads. They walk through the velvet darkness, very casual thumbs held to the street. Another ride. At the levee, where they were only earlier, they get out.

Here and there, along the expanse bordering the river, fires burn beside parked cars. Young nomads do dope, others make love, still others sleep outside or in ragged tents.

Still pilgrims, they walk away slowly—away from the scattered cars. The moon spills on the water, which shines like silk. In the midst of it are the small islands of sand. It's a brilliant night, like twilight.

As if by silent agreement, they've reached the island where they built the magic castle. They stand in awe before the silver-coated blackness of the water, the night breathes warmly on them.

Suddenly Manny removes his shirt, shoes, pants. The stabbing fear is gone completely. Naked, he plunges into the river. The others watch him running onto the small island. Theirs.

And then dashing along the water, Shell follows him, her dress clinging to her body.

The two, Shell and Manny, stand apart on the island.

From the levee, Cob watches them, clear in the bright night. Jerry looks from one to the other.

Shell raises her hand, a tentative wave.

Then Cob removes his clothes, he rushes, naked, across the water, emerging on the island. Now Shell is waving at Jerry, motioning him to come across.

Jerry only looks at them. They've stationed themselves in a wide triangle on the island. Cob, naked, on the extreme right of it; Manny, also naked, on the other extremity; and Shell, her dress glued with moisture to her body, in the center. As far as each can get from the others and still be close.

Then Jerry removes his clothes. He stands naked as if finally to plunge into the river to join them. But he doesn't move.

Now Manny waves at him. Even so, Jerry doesn't move. Then Cob waves.

Shell's world. The three, on an island. And Jerry . . . She waves urgently.

None of them moves, as if afraid to violate the mysterious revelation of this silent interlude on the island, their island.

Jerry's world. He looks at Shell. At Manny. At Cob.

Cob's world. He looks from one to the other. He feels the river air on his body.

Shell glances at the trees. They fan in a network of coarse lace. She waves again to Jerry, to join them on the island.

Jerry's world. The river, flowing to . . .

Shell hasn't removed her clothes. The wet dress renders her luminous and silver and lovely in the haze of moon. Once again she motions Jerry to join them.

The four stand like sentinels guarding isolated outposts.

Jerry looks at Shell, then quickly at Cob, and then at Manny.

Manny looks at Jerry, at Shell. Then at Cob. Manny's world. A sudden joy rent by a knife of darkness.

Cob looks at Shell, Manny. At Jerry. Then quickly at the shimmering black river.

Shell looks at Cob, Manny, Jerry.

They don't move. They stand apart in that distorted rectangle.

Shell.

Cob.

Manny.

Jerry.

Slowly Jerry wades into the water, joining them at last on the island.

For eternal moments within the vacuum of drugged time, they remain there. Then silently, again as if by signal, they wade across the water, to the bank. Cob, Manny and Jerry dress, ending the strange interlude. They feel the drug releasing them.

'We'll go back to my house,' Shell says. 'We can all stay there tonight.'

Shell lying next to him . . . Jerry imagines that. All of them, together . . . He looks at Shell; yes, he wants to lie next to her.

Thumbing again on the highway. A car stops. A youngman and a girl. A silent ride.

It's a radiantly clear night.

Out of the car. Walking up the hill to Shell's house. Hours have passed; sometimes it seems like seconds, sometimes like days. The effect of the drug is beginning to recede, like a tidal wave pulling back slowly, then swiftly, less slowly, more swiftly. The stars are regaining their aloof distance.

Inside Shell's apartment, in the center of the room are the beads, necklaces, the stones they played with earlier. The four look down forlornly at their playthings, almost stripped of the outrageous magic of the drug; it barely wafts the colors with brightness.

'I'm crashing, man,' Manny says; he lies on the floor. He's exhausted. For him this night's trip had not been finally good; there had been the shooting fear and desolation.

'We'll do some reds,' Shell says.

Time is assuming its dimensions within reality. A space of it has been gone through easily, but another—vaster—is approaching; and they need salvation from it:

Already Shell is holding the sleeping pills in her palm. Seconal. Again one glass of water. They sit on the floor drinking from it like communicants.

The sleeping pills pull them down quickly into a mellow, gentle sweetness. Determinedly, they refuse sleep.

Manny curls up on the floor like a child. 'I wish . . .' he mutters drowsily.

'What, man?' Jerry asks.

'I just wish,' he says. 'What do you wish, Cob?' he asks.

'I wish . . .' Cob stops. As if he dare not commit himself even to a wish. 'Nothing. You should never wish for anything.'

'Why not?' Manny mutters.

'Because . . .' Again Cob stops, words meaningless and superfluous even before they form.

'What do you wish for, Jerry?' Manny questions.

'I wish . . .' Jerry too blocks his words. His wish would test the drug's power to jar his world out of desolation. Tomorrow, in the muted house . . .

'I wish it was always pretty, like the drug,' Manny says, his eyes closing dreamily, mercifully forgetting for now the moments of lost apprehension, remembering the great joy. 'And you, Shell?'

'Nothing,' she whispers.

All barefoot, the boys shirtless, they fell asleep on the floor.

13

Abruptly Jerry woke.

In the bright invading glare of the morning desert sun, the lights inside are muted halos, colored fireflies—the room seems determined to retain a part of the drug's glow.

And it remains too within Jerry. He feels exhilarated. Alive! The others lie very still on the floor.

Jerry moves quietly on bare feet into the kitchen.

Riding the euphoria of hinted liberation, impulsively, with great care, he tears a sheet of paper into a heart. He places it on the cushion he slept on last night. He feels stunningly close to the others, finally his companions in the journey to expel the pall of death.

Then he walks quietly out of the house.

Hearing him leave—she had wakened but remained very quiet—Shell opens her eyes and sees the paper heart he left. She stares at it. Then slowly, tentatively, as if not committing herself totally to the action, she touches its jagged edges. Finally she allows her hand to rest fully on its surface.

Quickly, she withdraws it. She stands, brushing her hair with her fingers. Even at this time of waking, she looks glorious.

Manny is still curled up.

Lying on his side, long hair disheveled, Cob opens groggy eyes to a hostile world. He puts on the purple sunglasses quickly and looks around. 'Where's the other dude? I mean, like someone's missing,' he tries to obscure his quick awareness of Jerry's absence.

Shell points to the paper heart and watches Cob.

Cob looks quizzically at the heart. 'He left this?'

'Yes,' Shell answers.

Cob shrugs, ignoring the heart until Shell went into the kitchen. Now he barely touches it.

The voices woke Manny. 'What's that?' he asks.

Swiftly Cob withdraws his hand from the heart. 'A heart, what the fuck do you think it is?' he says.

'Like whose?' Manny asks sleepily.

'Jerry left it,' Shell says from the kitchen.

'Who for?' Manny asks.

'No one—he's just trying to put us on,' Cob dismisses quickly.

'Oh.' Manny peers curiously at it. 'The dude's too much, right?' he asks, as if to extract from their reactions the acceptable one.

But the others say nothing, as if they too are confused by the presence of the heart.

Now they're in the kitchen, Shell is making eggs, Cob is fixing coffee, Manny is placing dishes on the table.

'Where did he split to?' Manny asks.

'Probably hitched a ride to go feed his cats,' Cob says.

'He'll be back,' Shell says.

Finished eating, they gather the dishes, wash them, dry them together.

'Why do you think he's so uptight over letting us into his house?' Cob asks abruptly.

Shell says easily, 'Because he wants to keep two parts of his life apart—he's not sure which one he wants.'

'What parts?' Cob asks.

'His mother—and us,' Shell answers.

'But she's dead,' Manny says.

'Not yet—not for him,' Shell says.

'Fuck him if he doesn't want us in his house,' Cob says.

Quickly Shell says: 'We'll go for him.'

'Are you digging on him, Shell?' Manny blurts abruptly.

'She just wants to get into his head,' Cob says with finality.

Strange, incongruous laughter seizes them.

'Let's get it over with and go for the dude,' Cob tries to sound impatient. 'It'll take him all morning to get out here.'

Shell showers, changes into a bright yellow long dress. Beads gleam abundantly about her neck.

'You're beautiful, Shell!' Manny is assaulted by the radiant visual spectacle.

'So are you,' she says easily, deliberately diminishing his words. 'All angels are beautiful.'

Cob and Manny take turns showering.

Moments later—Cob driving, Shell in the middle, Manny on the other side—they ride down the hill to the highway. Stationed at regular intervals along it, long-haired youngmen and girls sell carnations, holding the radiant flowers to passing cars.

Cob speeds away from them.

'You think he's at that old house with the cats or at his sister's?' Cob asks.

'His old house,' Shell says decisively.

Jerry got there only moments earlier.

He stands under the icy chandelier in the living-room. Memories of his mother swirl about him. She sat there! She walked here! She moved down those very steps! She smiled, she talked, she laughed, she cried! Now there's the physical absence, the unyielding silence! . . . Feeling tears beginning without control (*Don't cry!*), he grasps frantically for the drug's anchor: *Even the severed branch grows again! Resurrection!* . . . Mother . . . He feels her gentle presence. Mother . . . the tears . . . *Even the severed branch grows again! Resurrection! Resurrection!* . . . He breathes more easily now. The tears that would have racked him have withdrawn. And so yesterday's life-asserting illuminations survived into the real world! he tells himself eagerly.

From within the still house, the two furry cats approach him slowly. Now they curl at his feet. Joining his anxiously embraced—determinedly seized—hint of peace? He bends down, petting them profusely, his face rubbing their fur. And then he sees the brown Burmese at the door. Not approaching, she merely watches him and the other cats with gleaming yellow eyes. Now she rushes up the stairs. To wait before the locked room, Jerry knows. He moves slowly up the stairs. The brown cat has disappeared. Jerry advances toward the closed room. His fingers barely touch the door's knob, the key. He withdraws his hand urgently and turns away.

Outside, Cob holds his hand steadily on the honk.

Jerry hears it. He knows it's them—he's glad they're here; he would have hitchhiked back to join them.

The honking continues outside.

Jerry rushes down the stairs. Once more—very quickly—he looks about the house. And suddenly, feeling strong enough, he knows what he has to do this morning: a powerful test of the drug's revelations, their lasting power within the world that contains death.

He runs out of the house, to his new friends. Manny sits in back with him.

'Now what?' Manny poses the inevitable question.

Jerry says quickly, 'There's somewhere I have to go.' Deliberately he withholds where from them.

'Sure, man,' Cob agrees.

Jerry gives him directions. Then, 'Stop here.'

Tall stones loom at the cemetery where his mother is buried.

Cob looks quickly at Shell. She frowns vaguely. Manny makes a disguised sign of the cross.

'Wait here for me!' Jerry calls. Quickly he gets out of the stopped car and rushes through iron-grilled gates into the cemetery.

Crosses. Statues. Urns. The props of death everywhere. He looks at the alive green velvet grass. He runs along the winding road to face his mother's grave, her death. Armed with yesterday's illuminations carried from the magic world, he has to know whether the black pain has been utterly contained. His mind repeats wordlessly, *Even the severed branch grows again! Resurrection!*

Her grave.

He pauses. The grass around it has not yet grown, the ground is leprous. He moves closer. He remembers: The canvased area under which they stood, he and his sister and the others who came to mourn; the box before them, sealed forever now.

Reaching it swiftly, he stares at the stone. Her favorite virgin guards it. The inscription reads: 'With The Greatest Love.' Desperately he evokes the words of yesterday's drugged liberation: *The severed branch! To grow again! The cycle of life! Resurrection!* He touches the stone. It's cold, hard, dead. Suddenly he remembers. At the hospital needles penetrated her veins in burst stars. Mother! So close in his memories, yet so irretrievably far within the black country of death. *Mother!*

And suddenly his whole body was seized by loss. Tears came beyond control.

'Mother!' he cries aloud—and knows that nothing has changed. The drug has not even assuaged the vicious pain of loss. And instantly the knowledge cuts into him like a million brutal knives, each carving out a severe wound into the desolate vulnerability.

Running, he flees the grave. Angrily he wipes away the tears. *Don't cry!* Then slowly, waiting for his eyes to dry, he returns to the car outside the cemetery.

Shell stares at him relentlessly.

Cob duplicates her look.

Accusing silence encloses him.

Cob still driving, they ride away.

Jerry feels a burgeoning depression, a huge despair. He feels cheated. Bitterness slices into him. Bitterness becoming rage. And yet there's this—he pulls the thought—even if the revelations of the drug changed nothing in the world ruled by death, even if the revelations were spurious, still the drug can dazzle him again. There's *that* of momentary Escape.

'Let's do some more dope!' he breaks the spell of silence.

Anxious to be released from it, the others join in approval. There's an instant mood of euphoria.

'Like the cat's a heavy doper now,' Cob laughs.

The day assumes a definite shape as they speed back to Shell's. It's a glorious, clear day. There's a delicious warmth in the air. Jerry's world. Anger recurs in roaring assaults.

Ahead and to one side of the highway, a barefoot long-haired youngman, smiling, stands selling carnations.

'I want some flowers,' Jerry says abruptly. His voice is cold.

'Shit, man,' Cob puts it down.

'He wants some flowers, let him get them,' Shell says firmly; the tone of Jerry's voice has alerted her.

'Shit, man . . .' Cob repeats.

'I want some fucking flowers,' Jerry says firmly.

Cob stops the car. Jerry jumps out. He approaches the youngman at the corner. The two face each other. They resemble each other uncannily—except that the flower vendor is smiling and Jerry is looking fiercely at him.

Jerry hears his own words: 'Those flowers are dyed.'

'Oooo-eee,' Manny says in the car.

And Cob understands what Shell sensed earlier.

'Sure—and they're pretty,' the youngman says, extending a bunch to Jerry.

'They're fucking ugly,' Jerry says, the meanness flowing. 'They look weak.' Suddenly he grabs the extended carnations, and he flings them bitterly into the street.

'What the hell . . . ?' the youngman protests.

Jerry stands by the curb watching as passing cars crush the flowers into pastel smears on the gray asphalt. The vulnerable part of him lies smashed on the street, dead.

Inside the car, he feels exhilarated. Victorious.

And Shell's smile, Cob's swift glance, a shake of Manny's head—they acknowledge it.

The car speeds away. Back to Shell's house.

In her apartment Shell is holding pinkish, gnarled pills, the color of faded roses. A different kind of mescaline from yesterday's. She takes a pill, passes the others to them. Each swallows one with milk from the requisite one glass.

Taped music prepares to receive the spell.

Tense, anxious, Jerry is desperate for the drug to possess him. Reality keeps pulling his mind to his mother's grave. From there it lunges to this. He rushed her to the hospital; he was in the ambulance with her, and he held her hand, his body quivering, anxious to give her his strength, his life. He pulls away from that burning memory, only to be devoured by this one. Her beautiful eyes had looked at him in panic . . .

Manny is the first to get off. A smile blesses his face as he welcomes the world of colors, pulsing music. He laughs uncontrollably. 'My old lady . . .' He can't stop laughing. 'My old lady, man . . . Diggit, I haven't been home since yesterday morning. I bet she thinks I turned myself in to the J.D. home, man! . . . I hope . . . I hope she misses the hell out of me!'

Shell too is getting off, her beauty radiates the joy of the drug.

And it's releasing the child in Cob. In wonder, he's studying the shattered images of a kaleidoscope. Now he passes it to Shell, and then he smiles warmly at Jerry. 'Like . . .' Cob begins uncertainly. 'Like here we are, man.'

'Right on,' Manny approves as if Cob has just solved a great riddle.

But Jerry is not getting off. He feels the gathering tension of the day, the frightened cat, the panicked yellow eyes. The grave. The grave. The locked room. Death. He stares at the colors in the room, demanding that they light up with magic, demanding they part to allow him entrance into the dazzling world. But nothing.

Cob passes the kaleidoscope for Jerry to share.

But to Jerry there is no magic. Not in the kaleidoscope. Not in the rocks, beads, or glass which Shell has spread again on the floor. It's been an hour since he dropped the mescaline.

He walks impatiently to the window. The warmth of the day has become heat. The yellow desert seems to be steaming.

He turns desperately to the others. For them the magic doors have opened wide. Their soft laughter indicates it. Occasionally they hold a rock to each other, admiring it, touching its beauty.

He knows for them it contains a piece of the dazzling universe. They pass it to him—and it's just a rock. Feeling a fathomless depression, he turns from them. . . . The grave, the frightened cat. The grave. Death. Urgently he goes to the kitchen. Anxiously he takes another hit of the mescaline, the kind he took yesterday, the slick, bright-red capsule.

Another half hour passes. More. Still, nothing.

Manny, Cob, and Shell are exploring the hidden universe contained within the room.

And then the door of the drug opens for Jerry.

But this time it didn't open gently. It was flung apart, and he was pulled savagely into the secret world. He felt his body jerk violently as if two powerful opposing forces had collided within him—and he heard a *Zoom!* But all that mattered was that he was in the dazzling world.

And, everything is radiant now! The violent entry has not altered that. Through the window the desert shifts in layers of dazzling beauty, as if lit by a golden light. But suddenly *Zoom!* again—a sound he does not so much hear as feel, an implosion within his mind. And the world funnels. But now again there's the beauty quickly. The sky, lowering, forms soft-blue parting panels. *Zoom!* The world spirals darkly. Then again it opens into the rainbow spectrum bathed in the drug's magic.

Jerry joins the others on the floor. They welcome him with extended beads, rocks, the kaleidoscope.

Suddenly, and time's boundaries are quickly eradicated, they're outside. Suddenly they're on the highway. Suddenly they're giggling inside a car that stopped to give them a ride.

Jerry stares at the face of the driver, a man. As before in the earlier stage of the drug, the face melts, but this time only into horrendous shapes. Jerry looks quickly away, at the dazzling sky. *Zoom!* The world closes, holds its breath, opens harshly. 'Where are we?' Jerry asks.

'Who cares?' Manny says.

On the suddenly hot, humid street. When did they get out of the car? *Zoom!* The world rushes at Jerry in a vortex. In a car again. The driver's face, again a hideous, menacing visage. Jerry frowns. Why, this time, does the drugged world contain so much that is ugly? *Zoom!* Out of the car.

A tangled maze, the streets have bunched up as if the world is painted on wrinkled paper. Cars melt into chrome dinosaurs. *Zoom!* In another, a speeding, car. When he exhales this time, Jerry spews out the twisted world.

'Man, that was dynamite shit we took! I am ripped!' Manny is saying. 'I bet that shit had some heavy acid and speed in it!'

Cob is giggling: 'I'm so messed up, I . . .'

Voices: 'Where shall we go?'

Where?   Where?

                                    Where?

                Where?   Here.

There.   There.

                                                      Here.

Suddenly Jerry wants to come down from the drug's soaring high. The world is rushing within his head. To dissipate the disorientation, he forces himself to laugh; his laughter comes back at him like a cry.

The others laugh.

Zoom! They're walking along a street. *Zoom!* They're inside a church.

'How did we get here?' Jerry asks.

'We hitchhiked, man!' Cob reminds him.

'Why are we in *this* church?' Jerry persists. It's the same church where—when was it?—they 'confessed'!

'Because you said this is where you wanted to come,' Manny reminds him.

Did he? Oh, yes. But *did* he? If so, why?

Zoom!

Jerry is standing before the altar. The martyred figure of the crucified Christ breathes, sighs in pain. Jerry feels crushed by sorrow for him. He sees Christ's blood flowing. He turns away desperately.

Zoom!

He's standing before the mosaicked window. The sun has brought it to life. The angel and the slain dragon. Jerry hears the dragon's howl. Or the angel's? *Who destroyed whom?*

Zoom! Before the altar again. He looks up, to the crucified Christ, up, to God, the culprit! *You killed him! And you killed my mother!*

Did he really shout those words? *Zoom!* He's standing before the mosaicked window. The angel is poised to slay . . . *Us!*

14

Outside the church.

Eeeeeeeeeeeeeeeeeeeeeeeeeeeeeeeeeeeeeeeeeeeeeeeeeeee!!!!!!!

Jerry sees the wind coming at him like a hideous bird, feels it clawing at his face, his eyes. Where can he look? Shell is standing before him. He studies her. Shell. Demonic. Beautiful. A divinely beautiful demon.

Zoom!

How did they get here? Time, space are shattered. They're in a giant drugstore. Smashed perfumed odors, spliced sounds, broken colors—instantly they accost Jerry. And people, menacing bodies dwarfed, melt along the store, which tilts.

The four go through turnstiles.

'I dig carnivals!' Cob approves the choice of store. He rushes happily to a display of cheap jewelry. Shell and Manny join him.

Jerry watches the three digging into the glass beads. *Zoom!* An amber film filters his eyesight darkening everything. *Zoom!* He's in a giant box filled with insane people in a howling angry world. Colors pull at him savagely—dyed quicksand in his mind, which is running, lost within itself in a jungle of clanging memories. His mother's death, the grave, the cat's eyes, the locked room, death!

Shell's world. She feels the beads luxuriously, discovers their pure inner shapes, so pure and crystal. Smilingly she holds out a fistful to Jerry.

He rejects them desperately.

Cob marches along the aisles of the store like a proud explorer; smiling, owning his private world.

Manny is whirling a display of sunglasses deliriously.

Eyes! Dead colored eyes! Jerry cowers against the enclosing walls. *Zoom!* Amber darkness, like the wing of a giant bird.

Zoom! They're outside. The streets are rollercoaster tracks. Jerry is laughing very hard, vainly trying with laughter to drive away the assaulting horror. The heat is like wet gauze pasted on his body.

Zoom! In and out of cars.

Zoom! Downtown El Paso. Streets crowded with strange people involved in a savage, arcane ritual to tear each other apart. Buildings angle as if to touch their shadows. A cacophony of clashing sounds! Where has the drug's beauty fled? Jerry wonders. Is he down, off the drug—and is this, finally, the real world? Trees in the old plaza shriek insanely.

He looks down at his hand. A skeleton! Terrified, he 'feels' himself running through the crowds, searching . . . What? What! . . . But he's not really running. He's walking with the others, all laughing.

'Outasite,' Cob is approving their trip, staring at people.

'Ooooo-eee,' Manny agrees happily.

Shell's world. Her face is tilted toward the clean sky, which smiles back at her.

Jerry grasps for a focus on reality, a focus to pull him out of the quicksand of roaring insanity: 'I've got to go feed the cats!' he says urgently. The words form like entities on his electrified mind.

'Sure, let's go to your house,' Cob says.

Frantic to get there—a haven—Jerry doesn't protest this time. The drug has abandoned him within a subterranean level beyond the outrageous beauty—fled—of the earlier experiences.

They walk along familiar streets grown sinister for Jerry. Houses seem coated over with colored moss. They walk through an eternity, until, finally—blessedly real in a sea of distortion— there it is:

The house!

His mother's house . . .

His house!

Cob's voice. 'We'll all come in.' He spoke the words softly, uncertainly. An entreaty this time? Has the house Jerry will not allow him into become a symbol of isolation for him? Or in a shaping conflict between them, has it become the immediate focus of vague victory?

The drug flowing powerfully within him, Cob does this impulsively. He touches Jerry, on the shoulder, doubling the entreaty of his words. His fingers remain there, lightly, but totally committed to the gesture: the enactment of earlier moments of rehearsal.

Slowly Jerry's own hand rises as if to cover Cob's on his shoulder. But instead he pulls away swiftly. He glanced at Shell, and her look was dark. The very vulnerability he has tried to cleanse himself of was seizing him again! He will not allow it.

Terrified, he backs farther away from Cob's touch.

Cob's world. Unexpectedly he hears his own words forming beyond control. 'I just wanted to touch you, man, because you looked so scared.'

'No!' Jerry backs away farther from him. 'No one can touch me any more!'

As if within his own drugged world a tension had unwound in Manny, he goes quickly to Cob. '*I'll* touch you, Cob! *I'll* touch you!' And he touches Cob's hands urgently.

Suddenly Jerry rushes into the house, closing, locking the door. Quickly! To be alone again with the lingering ghost of his mother! My mother and myself—alone! he thinks, as if with his life he can pull her from death . . . He pulls the bolt over the lock. Then—as if the house is issuing a commanding whisper to him from out of the pools of locked heat—he looks about it.

The house is a cave.

The brown cat is staring at him from within its depths.

'Stop looking at me like that!' Jerry shouts at the animal. 'I didn't take her away!'

The cat shrieks at him, body arched, hair on end.

Reality crashes on Jerry.

The cat flees.

Jerry wanders about the enormous house, searching out the cat, to explain . . . The other cats have come out, are looking curiously at him. Does he appear strange? Different? Both cats suddenly recoil from him. Why? The vibrations, almost electric, emanating from his body? His infectious panic touching them?

He's upstairs. Before the locked room. The brown cat isn't here. Does she realize . . . ? He looks away from the hugely vacant room.

He's searching other rooms in the house, a desolate, empty world. He pulls doors aimlessly, each opens with a sad sigh. What is he looking for? Oh, yes, the brown cat. But he keeps calling softly: 'Mother, Mother.'

Zoom! Another room. *Zoom!* The stairs. *Zoom!* His mother's room again. Closed against her death. He touches the door, touches the key. Memories scream! He covers his ears as if to crush the raid. He rushes away. *Zoom!* Still another room. A closet, the door parted slightly. He opens it. Darkness spirals, forms fingers grasping at him. Yellow eyes gleaming! The brown cat crouches on a dark shelf. He has to reassure her! He has to soothe her. Terrified, the cat lunges at him, claws ripping at his flesh. He looks down at his hands. Blood. He feels a gasp coming from his throat.

Then, the rushing madness: The house shrinks. Monster shadows squeeze out of every corner. Is there Escape from the world of this strange house? He can send a secret signal from the window. I'm lost! The stark, silent house. *Zoom!* He's looking out a window. Shell, Cob, Manny downstairs.

The doorbell!

Stairs curl at his feet.

Zoom! He's leaning against the door. 'What do you want?'

'Let us in, man!' He hears Manny's voice.

'No,' Jerry says.

'He's bumming,' comes Manny's voice.

'We have to get him out,' Shell says.

For them, the drug's spell has ended. And they realize that for Jerry the insane world has spilled into reality.

'I'll climb through a window,' Manny says.

'No, that'll freak him out worse,' Shell says with authority. 'He'll just run away.'

The somber, cold Cob is returning swiftly. 'If the dude wants to lock himself in his fucking house, let him.'

Through the closed door, Cob's voice grates like sand against Jerry's mind.

Shell says to Cob: 'We're the four angels.'

'What's wrong with being three again?' Cob says.

'Just a moment ago—when you wanted to touch him . . .' Shell begins, ambiguously. In accusation? Reminder?

Cob turns from her, as if to walk away. But he waits.

Shell knocks insistently but softly on the door. 'Jerry, it's Shell, let us in.'

Her voice. Shell . . .

'Let me in, Jerry,' Shell insists even more softly.

Jerry leans against the closed door.

Shell's voice: 'What you're into, man—you're having a bummer, and I'll help you out of it if you open the door. We'll rap, man; just rap.'

A wave of tenderness. 'Okay.' Jerry unlocks, unbolts the door, opens it. He faces Manny and Shell.

Shell glances into the enormous twilit house. 'Split with us, you can't stay here alone,' she tells Jerry.

Manny retreats slightly. Looking into the solemn house, he edged too closely into Jerry's threatening world.

'You're bleeding,' Shell says to Jerry.

Jerry withdraws his hand. He studies them. Then he sees Cob a few feet away. The dark sunglasses. The brooding face. *Death!*

Quickly Jerry closes the door, locking it again.

Manny's voice through the door: 'Goddamnit, man, open the fucking door!'

'Don't yell at him!' Shell's voice orders Manny. 'When you're on a bummer, you can't take it!—he'll never open the door that way.'

'How do you know about bumming, Shell?' Cob tosses at her. 'You ever bummed out, Shell?' He remembers acute pain in his mind.

'Man, I . . .' Shell begins, shifts abruptly: 'I know all about the *real* shit.'

Cob accuses harshly: 'You really want to help the dude, Shell—or you want to get into his head now, when he's freaking and it's easier?'

'Guess!' Shell flings at him.

'Shell's trying to *help* the dude!' Manny insists frantically; like yesterday, his own world is being threatened, but for him—as well as for Shell and Cob—the drug's effects have lapsed, and so the threat exists on the shore of reality.

'Is she?' Cob flings at him. 'Is she fucking trying to help him? Or just *get* to him?'

'Or is that *your* trip, Cob?' Shell counters.

'You are! Aren't you, Shell? You are trying to help the dude! We all are, aren't we?' comes Manny's desperate voice.

'Sure,' Shell says.

The harsh sound of their words storms Jerry's mind violently. He feels a spiraling disorientation . . . Death! Escape! To what? Death. No Escape! *Mother!* Death . . .

He slides against the wall. The house—his enemy—touches him.

He hears a window rattle.

A voice. 'The window's locked, Shell, I can't pry it open.' Manny's.

Another voice. 'Let's try the back door.' Shell's.

The back door! His means of Escape! Jerry rushes to it. *Zoom!* He's outside. *Zoom!* The world, sky, trees crash. Orange-white, the sun is setting. It attacks him with fierce white fire and heat.

He runs through the back garden, out the gate, which clangs.

Trapped echoes in his mind. Clang! Voices: 'He's running away!' Clang! 'Where is he?' 'We'll have to find him!' Clang! *Zoom!* And Cob's voice: 'Let the dude go!' 'No—we've got to find him!'

Voices left far, far behind. Perspiring, his clothes wet on his body, Jerry is running breathlessly through alleys—a hostile twisted jungle of gnarled shapes. The sun. Where is it now? Gone. Mother! *Zoom!* Night! Where is he? Houses crouch like frightened animals. *Zoom!* He remembers the brown cat! *Zoom!* Is it possible? Yes, without realizing it, he's run here. He's standing across the street from the hospital where his mother died. He remembers the ambulance, the corridors, her body, the needles in her arms, the scream from his soul . . . He smothers tears within him. Don't cry! He sits down wearily. *Mother!* No, he's not sitting down, he's running again. *Zoom!* A highway in the jungle!

Cars pass—their lights are a slow lighted cortege.

He stands on the curb.

And he's aware of the exposed, naked universe. Of its glaring hostile stars! Of whirling masses of angry space!

Zoom! He's in a car. Did he hitchhike? The man—who is he? He looks familiar.

'How far are you going?' Words issue from the man's mouth.

'Just ahead!' Jerry pronounces. He leans back in the car. He looks steadily at the man. 'Who are you?' he asks him.

The man studies him. He frowns. 'Why? Do I look familiar?'

'Do I?' Jerry hears his own words.

The man hesitates. 'I'm not sure.' He looks ahead.

Jerry's world. He's running in the forest of his mind.

'Are you all right?' the man asks him.

'Don't I look all right?' Jerry feels a blaze of anger.

'Of course,' the man placates him, 'you just seem a little . . . tired.'

'I am,' Jerry hears himself say, and now he feels an engulfing gratitude, kindness toward this stranger. 'I am, man, I am so tired.' He closes his eyes wearily, but even in the closed darkness the menacing black shapes attack. He opens his eyes. *Zoom!* A drive-in theater!—but didn't they just pass it? And there it is again. Are they driving in a straight circle? A straight circle. Past, present fusing in memory, his mind opens, closes, like a movie run on a circular machine, recurring. Is *any* of this real? Is he still locked inside the house imagining all this? The sky, the night, this man, the universe? Zoom! Jerry stares at the man. Who is he?

'Man, I'm bumming!' Jerry hears his words, a howl. He holds his head desperately in his hands.

Did the man understand? Or was it only the franticness of the words? 'You want to go to the hospital?' he asks quickly.

'No! That's where she died!' Jerry blurts. 'Just . . . please . . . drive.'

'Okay,' the man says.

Jerry's memory plunges suddenly into a dark pool; remembers a dark house near a bar. And a man surrounded menacingly by them—the four angels. 'Are you Stuart?' he almost shouts the words at the man.

The man says slowly : 'No.'

But Jerry is convinced. 'I'm sorry!' he shouts. And the meanness and savagery of last night, the night before—when was it?—the cruelty he's been courting to save himself, himself alone, attacks him. 'I'm sorry . . .'

'It's okay,' the man says. And softly : 'I think you must go to the hospital, I'll wait if you like.' He turns the car around in the middle of the highway. Stops for the oncoming traffic.

Suddenly Jerry rushes out of the car. No, he won't go to the hospital—to confront more memories of the paralyzing loss! He's running across the highway. Cars are honking. Brakes are like the shrieks of jungle birds. Where is he? Inside a drive-in theater. On the screen, giant faces! Garish colors. *Zoom!* He's running desperately from car to car! Another hostile jungle of staring strange faces within the cars, and he's peering into every car, every window, every face, looking for . . . His mother! The brown cat! His mother! And death!—to kill it.

Zoom! He's out of the drive-in. On the highway, hitch-hiking. *Zoom!* In another car. Violent shapes form on his mind. Where is Stuart? Was it Stuart? The car he's in is stopped before a train, which is unmoving, blocking traffic. *Zoom!* Jerry opens the door of the car, he's running again. Voices are calling out urgently to him. He's crawling under the stopped train. He's under it. Round steel wheels gleam blackly. Feeling a great weariness, he lies on the ground, under the train. His fingers touch the rails.

Voices! Yelling at him! And a lantern! A flashlight cutting at him like a threatening knife! 'The train's going to move any second now!' And the flashlight! The flashlight! He remembers: Another flashlight. The dark abandoned house by the bar ...

Zoom! He's crawling from under the train, menaced by the light. He's on the other side, he's running frantically. *Zoom!* A forest? Trees, hills. Vaguely he tries to remember where he is. Trees bend to grab him. He runs. The heat crushes him. There's a streetlight within the forest! He remembers the park where he became ... an angel. Why did he come here? A hill. He has to climb it. With great effort. It seems that hours pass and he's still climbing it. Then he's on top of it. Yes, it was here, the same spot, where he became an angel a million years ago.

He lies on the grass nearby. Desperately trying to swim out of the undercurrent of insanity, he grasps at the magic anchors which failed him earlier: *Resurrection! Even the severed branch grows again! Resurrection!* But the drugged illumina-tions have lost all their power. He closes his eyes, allowing the dark shapes which he cannot Escape. Then he begins to cry, tears released easily.

How long did he remain there, trembling, crying? A second, a minute, an hour, hours?—feeling the tears washing away the twisted horror. He opens his eyes. The world is slowly ordering its chaos, the clutch of the drug's madness is fading.

He looks around. The twisted drugged world has withdrawn.

He stands. He knows with infinite relief that his terrifying journey through the long tunnel of insanity has ended. He stares at the sky. The universe—remote, distant, unconcerned—no longer crushes him. The stars, indifferent, do not bless—but do not menace.

In the dark heat, he removes his wet shirt. The air touches him apathetically.

15

Lights in the dark park are mute halos in the stifling night.

Jerry feels a vast relief to be out of the twisted world—but with it, still another sadness, that the beautiful world of the drug turned against him: that beneath its outrageous wonder lies insanity and darkness.

He walks slowly down the hill, toward the street intersecting the park. Exhausted, he lies on the grassy incline. For a moment he feels a wafting of the drug's insanity. Zoom. But it lasts only a moment. The world is again anchored in reality.

Then without surprise he recognizes Shell's car. He doesn't even get up, they'll see him. Shell applies the brakes sharply. Jerry hears Manny's relieved: 'There he is!' He and Shell run from the car, left in the middle of the street. Cob does not get out.

'Are you all right, man?' Manny asks Jerry.

'Yeah, man, what . . . ?' Shell blocks a note of entreaty.

Jerry nods. 'I'm okay.'

Shell studies him carefully. Yes, the drug's bad trip is over for him, she knows. The fear-drained face is gone.

Cob sits in the back seat of the car. From the incline, Jerry glances at the purple-shielded eyes, and quickly away. 'How did you know where to find me?' he asks them.

'It's on the fucking *radio*,' Manny says excitedly. 'When you ran away from us, we split and got Shell's car. Then we heard it on the radio—that some freaked-out dude tried to run under a train near the park!' Manny can't conceal a note of admiration in his voice.

136

Shell says to Jerry: 'You came here because this is where we met and you knew we'd look for you here.'

'Maybe,' Jerry says.

On the street, honking cars are protesting the blocked traffic.

'Come on!' Shell says, but she looks uncertainly at Jerry, as if she's not sure he'll come with them.

He follows them into the car. Manny sits quickly in front with Shell. Jerry sits in back with Cob. They drive away.

Imprisoned behind the dark sunglasses, Cob will not even glance at Jerry.

Is he remembering the strange interlude between them when he touched Jerry? Belatedly, as if reality is splicing the sequential order the drug destroyed, Jerry wants to explain to Cob those moments of rejected touching, explain that within the quagmire of insanity he had felt vulnerability then like an open wound (and was that all?!), that the touch of another would have seared him with pain. But Cob seems locked irretrievably within a cage of anger.

'Where are we going?' Manny forms the crucial question.

'To the old house by the bar, we're right near it, and I've got some hash,' Shell says, ordering her voice to sound natural.

Jerry remembers the violent whirlpool of blackness of that house. But he doesn't protest going there, as if he must now proceed to face himself in judgment.

Manny is forcing himself to laugh gaily. 'This dude, man, he's running under the train, man, diggit?—and all those straights are freaked out; and . . .' Manny's world. Insistently: We're together again, not alone. The four angels!

Jerry's world: We're hopelessly apart now. And do I want that?

Cob's world: A tension. A sense of exposed vulnerability. A ritual of power to be performed, to heal that raw wound with assertive strength.

Shell's world: Bewildered violence.

Again, the wing of the drug's madness brushes Jerry as they park before the gray, sorrowful house, the wooden X's across the windows signaling its doom. But this time the disorientation lasted the length of a desperate sigh.

Through the boarded window, they move into the darkness of the old house. Ghosts of their experiences within it stir: Stuart, the two men . . . Heat crouching along the corridor captures them instantly.

In the main room: Huddled shadows protected from each other's scrutiny by the hot entombing darkness, they sit on the floor.

Jerry's eyes move automatically to the transom; to the dead bird trapped there.

Shell is constructing a pipe for the hash. Finished, she passes it to Manny quickly, as if anxious to re-link the invisible chain, weakened, among them. Manny draws on the pipe, passes it to Cob urgently to complete the binding circle swiftly, Cob draws —and still without looking at him, he passes the pipe to Jerry.

Jerry holds it, he doesn't draw from it.

'You're afraid!' Cob attacks him eagerly; his anger can't wait any longer. His words snap within the charged mood. 'And it's just hash!'

Yes, Jerry's afraid it may stir the twisted world again, even though the earlier times it had no effect; his mind still feels raw from the hideous trip. Still, he wants to thwart Cob's anxious judgment of him. But he doesn't draw from the pipe.

'If you can't cope with the fucking dope . . .' Cob builds his attack on Jerry—an attack catapulted by the memory of the strange interlude of thwarted touching earlier?

'You're the one that can't cope with it, Cob,' comes Shell's voice in the darkness. Cob's anger is charging the room electrically like a naked live wire.

'What the fuck does that mean?' Cob's voice is hoarse.

'You copped out when Jerry bummed,' Shell says easily— whether accusing him or merely taunting him.

'Yeah, you fucking did,' Manny says. 'You were gonna split.' The accumulated tension of days is shaping at last; dark fog gathering from the ocean of their minds.

'When I . . . !' Cob begins to blurt. 'When I . . . he . . .' He flounders. 'I never cop out,' he regains cool control.

'It was a cop-out,' Shell says firmly. 'Jerry's one of us.'

'Is he?' Cob lashes.

In the darkness Jerry faces him. Finally, defiantly, he draws from the pipe. Waits. Tensely. Moments of terror; he remembers the monstrous flight into his mind earlier. But he feels in control. He draws from the pipe again.

Shell smiles at him.

But only because by his action he put Cob down? Jerry wonders.

'And you, Shell,' Cob strikes, 'you didn't cop out, did you? Because all you wanted was to get into his head all along—but he split,' he moves to create a wedge between her and Jerry.

Is he right? Had he been merely a part of their—Shell's—relentless pursuit of black experience? When she first saw him, crying in the park . . . ? Or had she really wanted to jolt him into an unfeeling strength, like hers? Had she tried truly to help him earlier today out of the quicksand of insanity? Or had she merely known that then was when he would be most vulnerable? Jerry looks at Shell for answers.

Her beautiful face is a dark, inscrutable mask.

'Shell wanted to *help* the dude,' Manny insists, as if otherwise he too will suddenly become an object for scrutiny, like Stuart.

Then Shell's calm voice enters the darkness: 'You feel threatened, don't you, Cob?'

'Yeah, man,' Manny says. 'You're always fucking threatened. By Jerry. By me. By your sister . . .'

'Don't call her my sister!' Cob shouts fiercely.

'That's what she is, man; face it.' Shell's voice is dull.

Yes, face it, Jerry thinks. That's all there is. To face It.

'She's . . .' Cob begins.

'A threat to you like everyone else,' Shell finishes in accusation. 'And you're afraid, Cob.'

'Of everyone, Cob!' Manny reacts to the finally released undercurrent of tension. 'Especially of Shell.'

'Afraid!' Cob reacts in anger. 'Shit! You're the one that's afraid, Manny—running to your old lady, who hates your guts . . .'

'You shut up, Cob!' Manny yells. It's as if during the days together as angels they've existed on a field of explosives requiring only the touch of a match to consume them in rage.

'And *you're* the one that's threatened, Shell,' Cob continues, a note of harsh warning permeates his voice.

Shell's words are cold, pronounced almost hypnotically like a strange prayer. 'No one, and nothing, threatens me, nothing scares me, nothing in the world, not you, not anyone, not any thing.'

'No?' Swiftly, Cob stands.

Fiercely, Shell stands to face him. 'No!'

'We'll see!' Cob assaults.

'Go ahead and try!' Shell moves for a showdown, long postponed.

'All that shit about how you're too strong to cry . . .' Cob derides.

'You think you can make *me* cry, man?' Shell asks with contempt.

'Yeah—because I've been into your head all along, Shell, and I know what scares you,' Cob threatens darkly.

'Try,' Shell challenges coldly.

'You're a fucking dike, Shell,' Cob says with viciousness. 'A dike!' he tosses the word with relished loathing.

Jolted by the open declaration of war, Manny and Jerry stand too.

'That's why you only want to bum out dudes, never chicks,' Cob lunges. 'Because you're a fucking dike.' Again infinite loathing coats the last word. 'You don't want cock, man, you want cunt.'

Automatically Shell touches her breasts, full, desirable. Then she laughs in Cob's face, laughs loudly, shaking. 'You really think *that's* going to scare *me?*—you think *that's* going to make *me* cry? Oh, man, you are too fucking much!'

'If you're not a dike, prove it, Shell,' come Cob's words.

Shell's laughter stops, as if sliced abruptly with a sharp knife. Then, as if forcing a connection within her, she resumes the derisive laughter.

Manny stares at Shell, at her breasts shaking with intense laughter. Instantly Cob's words released a pressurized under-current—Manny feels the diluted tension funnel with urgent swiftness into desire, there from the first and throughout, frustrated constantly.

Jerry is engulfed by the instant sensuality released by Cob's last words. A physical force seems to pass suddenly among them. There's an isolated intensity as if a powerful camera that has merely been scanning them has suddenly zoomed in on their emotions.

In surprise, Manny hears his own rash words, pulled out by desire. 'Yeah, Shell, prove it.'

Jerry whirls to face Manny.

'What the fuck does that mean, stupid?' Shell aims at Manny.

'Don't call me stupid!' Manny shoots back.

'He means just what he fucking said,' Cob says to Shell. 'You've laid all this heavy shit on us that you're the fucking first angel because you're so strong and tough, and you're the fucking leader, well, diggit, man, *I'm* the leader of this fucking game, and it's called "Cry, Shell." '

'Bull*shit!*' Shell laughs at him. 'We'll see who cries first. I told you, you don't scare me!'

'But this will!' In a sudden violent movement Cob rips the front of her dress, exposing her breasts. She wears no under-clothes.

Not reacting, Shell did not even flinch.

Manny stares at her bared breasts. Beautiful, naked, full, firm. His mouth opens automatically.

Wanting her, Jerry too stares at Shell.

'Take her, Manny!' Cob turns to him quickly. The gathered violence rushes turbulently.

Manny advances as if hypnotized by the bared breasts.

Only Shell's intense breathing reveals her anger. Her breasts rise, fall. But she stands very still.

Fascinated, Manny touches her nipples tentatively.

Jerry moves towards Manny. But he doesn't know whether he intends to stop him or to join him. He hears a shrill shrieking in his head—the wail of fused anger and desire.

Like a champion awaiting the exact moment of vulnerability to strike, Shell stares at Manny.

Rashly, Manny cups her breasts, one in each hand, squeezing them experimentally.

Shell winces. Her eyes close for a moment, as if to shut out a deeper darkness.

Swiftly, circling her like a cunning animal, Cob pulls her dress down.

Naked in tatters, she looks savagely beautiful.

Jerry moves automatically closer to her.

'Now prove you're not a fucking dike!' Cob shouts at her, moving for total control, the total vanquishment of her. 'Are you going to cry, Shell?'

Manny's fingers are moving clumsily on her body, edging in hypnotized fascination toward the parting between her legs, the soft triangle lightly brushed with hair.

In a movement belied by her delicate beauty, Shell pushes him violently away. Manny reels against the wall.

Instantly Cob is on her. Enraged, he wrenches her hands behind her, his knee at her back, pushing her toward Manny. 'Fuck the bitch!' he orders Manny.

Angry—and aroused—Manny unbuckles his pants quickly. His cock is already hard, throbbing expectantly, erect.

'Fuck her!' Cob calls.

Jerry moves. Again he's not sure whether it's to block Manny or take her himself. Or merely with motion to stop the shrieking in his mind.

'Okay!' Shell shouts. 'Okay! I'll ball you! But let me go!'

Cob doesn't release her. 'Fuck her, Manny!' he shouts, ignoring her words.

'Let her go,' Jerry says evenly. The shrieking subsides.

Cob continues to wrench her hands.

'Yeah, let her go,' Manny says. 'She fucking said she'd ball us.'

'But she won't,' Cob says. A note of desperation.

'Let her go,' Jerry insists.

Cob releases her.

Shell rubs her wrists. She stands in tatters before them. Perspiring bodies in the black heat. Then she strikes coldly: 'You first, Cob.'

Jerry feels resentment, anger.

'*You* prove I'm not a dike, Cob.' Shell's voice is in total, frightening control.

Cob turns to Manny, who still stands with his pants to his knees, his cock rock-hard, ready.

'Fuck her!' Cob says urgently.

'Why don't you want to go first, Cob?' Shell's words lacerate.

And Jerry understands, clearly. He remembers: Stuart, and the two men in the glare of the slaughtering flashlight. 'Yeah, man,' he hears his own words aimed deliberately at Cob, 'Why don't you go first?' He surrenders totally to the meanness: 'Are *you* afraid, Cob?'

'I'll go first!' Manny says eagerly, not understanding. He holds his cock impatiently in his hand.

'No, man,' Jerry blocks him. 'Cob has to go first.'

'Go ahead, Manny!' Cob yells.

'You first, Cob,' Jerry insists coldly. He still blocks Manny.

Shell's nakedness challenges Cob. He looks away from her.

'You first, Cob,' Shell repeats, and her smile attacks him.

Cob takes a step toward her. Then he turns away quickly. 'Go ahead, Manny!' he pleads.

The heat twists the darkness into strangling knots about them.

Then Manny frowns, understanding vaguely. 'No, Cob, you first,' he joins the attack on Cob.

Shell smiles triumphantly. Now her words crack like a whip lashing at Cob: 'Come on, motherfucker! . . . You can't, can you? Because you're fucking scared!'

Cob slaps her across the face.

Jerry grabs his hand. 'Don't do that!'

Shell laughs in Cob's face. Then she turns angrily to Jerry: 'Let him go! I don't need you or anyone else to protect me!'

Stung, Jerry releases Cob.

'You're afraid, Cob,' Shell aims to slaughter. 'Because you're a fucking faggot.' Quickly she adjusts her ripped clothes.

'Don't!' Cob reacts as if to hit her again, this time with his fist.

Now it's Manny who holds him, twisting his arms behind him.

Shell moves swiftly before Cob: 'Now *you*! *You* prove I'm wrong!'

Cob looks away.

Then in imitation of his violent gesture on her, Shell tears Cob's shirt from the front.

Manny holds him more tightly.

Rage, anger—a burning fever seizes Shell. In swift powerful movements she rips Cob's shirt into strips—and she ties his hands behind him. Her sudden, bewildered accomplice, Manny still holds him tightly.

Jerry is an uncommitted witness.

Relying on sudden motion, on shaping the whirling violence quickly before it assaults her—quickly seizing time—with incredible strength, Shell forces Cob onto the floor. He turns, struggles, resists.

His pants still lowered to his knees, his cock still aroused, ready, anxious, Manny sits on Cob's upper thighs to restrain him. Now Cob lies face down on the floor.

Then Shell's words form: 'Fuck him!' she orders Manny.

Manny looks down in bewilderment at Cob's prone body. Cob makes a jerking motion. Shell presses her total weight on his shoulders, restraining him. Manny looks at her.

'Fuck him!' Shell commands Manny, who seems again suddenly dazed, hypnotized.

And then with a sound that is laughter and panic, anticipation, desire, release, Manny pulls at Cob's pants, exposing his naked buttocks. Then he flings his body on Cob's twisting thighs while Shell still holds him powerfully, and he pushes clumsily against Cob's body.

Shell yells fiercely at Manny: 'Rip the hell out of him!'

Then the twisting movements of Cob's body stop abruptly.

Savagely, Manny lunges into him.

Pain exploding deep in his body, Cob yells.

Jerry is staring at Shell.

Still holding Cob, she looks up quickly, as if desperately searching an unblemished sky. At the moment of Manny's savage entering of Cob and Cob's shout of rending pain, she closed her eyes, wincing, her own body contracting as if in vicarious—remembered—pain.

Manny pumps into Cob.

Suddenly Shell leans over Cob, and she shouts angrily at him —but as if to someone else, a surrogate figure: 'How do *you* like it, goddamnit? How the hell do *you* like it! Bastard! Bastard!'

Jerry stares fixedly at Shell out of control, her voice waning, becoming weary. This act of violence—what substitute revenge for her?

Manny's pumping increases, his breathing is audible—even over Cob's sudden sobs. Manny pushes, hard, harder. . . . Then very slowly, in bewilderment, the terrible franticness and urgency released, he withdraws. He looks at Shell and frowns.

She turns away from him, faces Jerry. 'Now you!' she commands him.

Cob lies curiously still and unprotesting on the floor. Numbed by the pain? Surrendering? What?

Jerry looks at Shell's exposed body. Then he glances quickly at Cob's. Confused desire mixes with nausea.

A conquered warrior, Cob remains on the floor.

'Fuck him!' Shell yells at Jerry.

Jerry takes a step toward Cob. Then he retreats. Resurging momentarily, the violent part of him lies shattered in a pool of drugged insanity.

Manny stares at Shell as if stunned by his own act. Then he looks down at Cob. 'My mother *does* love me, Cob,' he whimpers bewilderedly.

'*Fuck him!*' Shell commands Jerry. 'He'll dig it, that's what he's wanted all along! He's a sick bastard!'

'It's you who are sick, Shell,' comes Jerry's voice.

Shell reacts as if slapped. Her long hair whips across her face.

16

Slowly, still dazed, Manny kneels over Cob, untying him. But Cob remains on the floor as if he can't—won't—yet face the new reality. His sobbing subsided as if it had never happened.

'And what about you?' Shell strikes back at Jerry. 'When we met you, you were whimpering. *That's* why I made you the fourth angel—to teach you how to stop crying . . . And when I met Cob and Manny, I knew . . .'

'*Was* that the reason, Shell?' Jerry forms the obsessive doubt Cob had voiced earlier. 'Or do you just dig . . . ?' Yet minutes before, she had attacked Cob for abandoning him in his drugged nightmare.

She stops his words sharply, repeats emphatically: 'To teach you how to stop crying! Because *that's* the sickest shit!'

'And all I found out is that I'm as rotten as you,' Jerry hears his words.

'No, not yet!' Shell warns ambiguously.

'But I'll control the rot, Shell,' Jerry thwarts her unclear threat. 'I'll try to,' he adds slowly, remembering the excitement of the violent encounters, an anesthetic numbing his own pain.

Shell stands angrily before him. Even now, she exudes a fierce sensuality. 'Then you'll always be weak,' she says ferociously. 'And what it's all about is to be strong! . . . Cob? Manny?' She glances at them—that glance, the uttered names, as if to explain to them what their strange initiation was about.

Adjusting his clothes, Cob stands. He rubs his wrists. He won't face Shell or Manny—or Manny him. Stunned, the two merely wait to react to the reality that crushed them earlier.

'Maybe,' Jerry says. He remembers the extreme vulnerability that thrust him into the twisted country of insanity. 'Yes, that too. But maybe it's also controlling the cruelty inside yourself.'

'Then you're fucked,' Shell says wearily.

'Why, Shell?' Manny asks out of the daze. He's buttoning his pants bewilderedly to shut out the immediate past.

Automatically: 'My father . . . !' Shell shoots the two words. She blocks the rest determinedly. The Shell of icy control returns. 'Because you've got to be strong, that's all,' she whispers. Then loudly, 'And that's *all* we've done—get stronger!' she insists. 'You, Manny!—letting your mother screw you over and going back to her all the fucking time for more shit . . . But no more!'

'She really loves me,' Manny insists.

'God damn!' Shell laughs brutally. 'God *damn*! You are really something else if you believe that!' She turns to Cob: 'And you, Cob, with all your bullshit. You've let your sister . . .'

Rendered totally vulnerable now, Cob says slowly: 'She's not my sister. Janet's just some chick my mother picked up in that bar at the corner and is hung up on . . .'

Jerry sighs.

'Oh, man,' Manny says.

Shell holds her breath, exhales slowly.

'Cob . . .' Manny begins, but he can't finish, he can't face him.

Seizing the exact moment, Shell shouts: 'Look at Cob, Manny! Face him! Goddamnit, face it all! You've got to prove you're stronger now, not weaker!'

Manny's world: *I'm afraid!* 'I wanted *you*, Shell, not Cob, you pushed me to . . .' He thrusts words into the empty house.

Shell says softly: 'I know, Manny,' at least for now releasing both him and Cob from the wounding knowledge. 'And that's why you *can* face him,' she insists. 'Now look at him, Manny.' Her words are hypnotic.

Responding abruptly to her powerful challenge to become strong, and her offer to withdraw judgment of the violent act, Manny faces Cob.

'Face *him*, Cob,' Shell's soft voice comes. 'Prove it meant nothing.'

Quickly Cob faces Manny.

'Now look at me,' Shell's voice almost implores.

Cob does.

Shell breathes easily. She's putting back her shattered world. 'And now you, Jerry.' She faces him nakedly as an antagonist.

Shadows within shadows, the two confront each other.

'It wasn't the drug that bummed you out—it was you!' Shell hurls at him.

'Whatever it was, it's over,' Jerry says quickly. But he feels the drug's black wing touch him, hears its desolate howl.

'Maybe, maybe not. Maybe you're still on a bummer, but you don't know it,' Shell says viciously.

Jerry shakes his head, attempting to shed the wailing blackness. 'No—my head's together now, maybe more than it's ever been before.'

Shell's words form like cold bullets. 'Let's find out, man. Let's go to your house. And to that locked room you won't face.'

The house. It flashes into Jerry's mind as it was earlier today, in whirling dark caverns, caves of emptiness, a forest of shadows. The unopened room.

'Yeah, let's go to your house, man,' Cob's words invade the darkness abruptly. His voice is again threatening, sinister. He must prove he hasn't been weakened, and that proof will deprive the violent act of the harsh meaning Shell has already conditionally withdrawn. He stares at Jerry through shielded eyes.

Manny retreats slightly. A part of him wants to block the inevitable, which Shell is already voicing like a sentence.

'Let's go to your house now, Jerry,' she repeats.

'No,' Jerry says quickly.

'Yeah, man. Now.' And Manny too joins them. The exposed weakness screams to be slaughtered.

'You'd have to force your way in,' Jerry hears the declaration of war bolting out of him.

149

'Okay,' Shell whispers.

'Okay,' Cob repeats.

'Okay,' Manny echoes.

Within the muggy silence Jerry moves slowly to the transom. Carefully he removes the crushed dead bird trapped there. He lays it softly on the powdered cement disintegrating from the fireplace. Then soundlessly he moves away from them, out of the room. His footsteps echo, loud, in the magnifying darkness along the corridor.

'He's gone,' Manny says in surprise.

Cob stares into the black hall.

'No!' Shell asserts. 'He can't leave.'

Silence. Within it they strain to hear the sound that will assure Jerry's exit: the pushing of the boards at the window. Nothing. They know he's waiting, undecided.

'He's the fourth angel,' Shell says firmly.

The unbearable heat trapping them; the dark heat waits silently.

No further sound. And so Jerry is still by the boarded window. In the dark room, straining shadows wait.

'He'll come back,' Shell repeats.

And then it comes : the sound of the boards.

'He's gone,' Manny sighs.

Outside, the dark house looms like a huge gravestone behind Jerry. His pace quickening, he begins to run away from it as if it, and the desperate ghosts passing through it, may summon him back. One block. Another. Another street. His life stretches like a plain before him.

Then the bright lights of a car, moving slowly, attack him from behind.

'Get in, man,' Shell calls softly. She's driving, all three sit in front.

'Leave me alone,' Jerry says. He pauses, he doesn't want them to think he's running away from them.

The crystal web of white light containing him, the car moves slowly.

150

Manny calls: 'Come on, man; you still bumming?' His voice, its tone, an eery imitation of Shell's.

'Get in, man,' Cob's cold voice insists.

Jerry doesn't answer. Avoiding the binding stare of the headlights, he crosses the street. The city swims in dark heat.

Suddenly Shell accelerates the car, the motor growls angrily. The car disappears.

Jerry begins to run. On Montana Street, he hitches a ride with two youngmen. Now he's out of the car—and immediately, he's running again.

And there it is finally: his needed refuge, his mother's house. White in the clear night. And within that spectral house, the locked room.

Holding his breath, he walks slowly up the stairs leading to the white columns. Angrily he pushes away a tumbleweed clutching at the porch. The drug's madness whispers to him, withdraws. He unlocks the front door. He stands in the dark hall. Will the shadows twist him back into the mad vortex? No. Inside, there's an ordered reality. Lights from a car outside scatter on the chandelier, fragmenting it into a shattered piece of ice. Entombed silence. Shadows float on the closed black heat. The veil of darkness lifts slowly as his eyes grow accustomed to the sealed night of the house.

The two furry cats appear. He touches them tenderly. But the brown one, where is she?

Now he sees her, two yellow eyes blaze unreally out of the dark.

Quickly the amber eyes disappear.

Jerry feels the cat's desolation, his own—and the presence of the dark, locked room—electric.

Footsteps outside!

He left the front door unlocked! He rushes back.

Cob, Shell, Manny are running up the stairs.

Shell opens the door.

Jerry confronts them. 'You're not coming in!' he says firmly.

'We are,' Shell says quietly. 'We have to.'

'Leave the dude alone,' Manny vacillates.

Shell turns on him. 'You're still weak!' she accuses.

'No, Shell,' Manny says. 'It's just that . . . he don't want us in his house, man.'

Jerry blocks the door.

'He's got to,' Cob says. The memory like broken glass buried in him, he remembers the moment of attempted, thwarted touching—here—which triggered the earlier confrontation.

'Yeah,' Manny retreats, 'like he's got to.' He knows, just as Cob knows, that Shell may again unleash the unwanted verdict on them.

Jerry begins to close the door.

Suddenly Cob pushes against it. And then, with a whimper of protest, rage, despair, Manny joins him. Jerry pushes back ferociously. And then Shell joins Cob and Manny forcing the door open.

They spill into the hall. The heat ambushes them.

Jerry moves back quickly.

Appearing suddenly, the brown cat stares defiantly at the invaders with glowing eyes.

To drive away her accusing stare, Cob shrieks: *'Neowwww-wwwwwwweeeeeee!'*

The cat shrieks back in terror.

'God damn you!' Jerry assaults Cob. Until he felt his fist aching and felt Cob's fallen sunglasses under his foot, only then did he realize he had struck Cob across the face.

Cob advances menacingly: 'You son of a bitch! You fucking bastard!' All the anger, the mysterious accumulated tension explodes.

'Don't fucking call me that!' Jerry shouts back.

Losing control: 'Leave him alone, Cob!' Manny yells.

Knowing that his mother's room will become the object of their insane invasion, Jerry runs up the stairs. Shell and Cob rush after him. The cats scatter in panic. Upstairs, the heat breathes even more fiercely. Jerry stands before the locked room, to block his own and their entrance. His body is cold, a cold shell in the pool of angry heat. Manny remains on the stairs, looking up at them, not committing himself fully to the invasion.

Shell shouts suddenly to Jerry: 'Unlock the fucking door! Face the goddamn room!'

Jerry's anger uncoils, snaps. 'Don't call it a goddamn room.'

'A goddamn room!' Shell shouts. 'Just a room you won't face!'

'Shut up!' Jerry yells at her.

Shell sees the key in the door. 'You've got to go in, Jerry,' she says softly.

'Leave me alone!' Jerry yells.

'You've got to face it!' Shell says.

'Alone! I'll face it alone!' Jerry shouts back.

'No you won't! You know you won't!' Shell insists.

'Now!' Cob yells.

Shell attempts to lunge past Jerry.

He moves to block her.

Cob grabs him.

Shell unlocks the door, flings it open.

Cob pushes Jerry into the room.

On the stairs, Manny is whimpering almost soundlessly: 'Leave . . . him . . . alone.'

Shell runs into the room. She finds the light switch, snaps it on. The room reels in light, shooting each object starkly into reality.

The room! The empty bed! A bed of death now! The empty bed which contained her body! Jerry looks at it, then quickly away, his heart choking.

'Look at it, man!' Shell yells at him. 'It's just a room now!'

Jerry sees Shell's taut outstretched body—and he remembers the darkest moment in his life. His mother breathing harshly! Tubes and needles a hideous network about her body! And suddenly in one bolting instant as if the accumulated seconds of her whole lifetime had gathered to rush out, her body convulsed fiercely, her hands, her legs were thrust out violently, her mouth opened uttering one last unscreamed scream as blood gushed from her lips! *What did she feel! Did death hurt!*

'*Mother!*' Jerry screams now, and feels the scream ripping his body. '*Motherrrrr!!!!!*'

Covering his ears, cowering against the balusters, Manny echoes Jerry's scream softly : 'Mother . . .'

Assaulted by the savage shout, Shell and Cob back away from Jerry and slowly out of the room.

The scream over, his face wet with perspiration and tears, alone now, Jerry stands quietly over the empty bed. As if the knowledge had been torn out by the scream, he knows: She's . . . dead. The word forms for the first time. He closes his eyes. My mother is dead. He opens his eyes, and he looks at the bed which he knows now will be empty forever.

Outside, Manny still crouches on the stairs. He whimpers over and over : 'Mother . . . Mother . . .'

Cob behind her, Shell stands over Manny—their shadows cover him. Shell's voice is emotionless, flat. 'Can't you understand she hates you, Manny?' she asks him softly.

'Leave us alone!' Manny shouts.

The heat is still, like stagnant water.

Shell's words continue softly. 'She hates you, Manny, she calls the pigs to bust you, she hates you, Manny.'

'She doesn't!' Manny yells.

'Manny, she throws you out of the house whenever she has a new lover.' Shell's soft voice is almost a whisper.

'Shut up, Shell!' Manny shouts.

Now Shell's words tumble violently into the cascading darkness. 'She hates you, she hates you!'

'I know it!' Manny shouts hysterically from the steps. 'Goddamnit, Shell, I know it!'

As if Manny's admission has calmed her mysteriously, Shell seems suddenly spent. And then she voices her final verdict on him and Cob: 'And you did want Cob, Manny; and Cob wanted Jerry.'

Cob walks past them, down the stairs.

Clinging to the balusters, Manny stutters: 'Shell . . . Shell . . .
Why are you so *mean?*'

Shell feels the dark heat like a hundred choking hands.
'Mean? Mean! Because I made you face . . . Because I . . .' Control shatters. She shouts: *'My old man fucked the hell out of
me when I was eleven! He spit on his goddam prick so he could
get it into me! And my old lady pretends she was too fucking
drunk to know what happened!'*

'I'm sorry, Shell,' Manny whispers, almost curling up on the
floor.

Now Jerry stands on the landing of the stairs.

'Sorry, shit!' Shell yells. She looks up at Jerry, calm now,
strangely calm; down at Manny; at Cob, who stands in the
desolate hall. 'I'm strong now! I've never cried since then—I
cried enough to last my whole fucking life. And I'll never
fucking cry again! Diggit: because I forced myself to look at
the shit—the way *you* have to!' she addresses them all. 'I bled,
I fucking bled—and I kept the bloodied towel; so I could face
it constantly, look at it, recognize it! And know how much they
hate me! *Face it!*' she shouts at them.

'You haven't faced yourself, Shell,' Jerry's cold voice calls
down to her.

She turns away from him. She walks quickly down the stairs.
Then defiantly she faces Jerry.

'You're like them now, Shell; your cruelty is just like theirs
now,' he accuses her—and himself? He'll remember, forever,
the brutality which charged him too. He looks down at Shell, a
shadow trapped in shadows. Yet . . . the radiant Shell released
gloriously by the drug. The Shell fascinated by toys, bright
colors, mystic aphorisms. Shell. The child . . . And out of the
forced invasion, yes, he faced the locked room. To accept death
. . . Was she right! But Manny, whimpering on the stairs . . .
And Cob . . . Cob, so frighteningly silent. Jerry calls: 'Cob . . .
I'm . . . sorry.'

As if that were all required to release the traumatized fear,
Cob's body begins to tremble. Bewildered, frightened, he hunts

about him on the floor for his shattered dark glasses. 'I . . . lost
. . . my . . .' he sighs. Finding them, he puts them on. He stands.
Through the smashed web of plastic, the world of this dark
house is even more twisted.

'You're all weak and sick!' Shell shouts at them. Her words
scatter the heat; it gathers about them with renewed ferocity.
'Why don't you cry? Cry! Show how fucking weak and lost
and sick you are! Well, I'm not, man! Because I've conquered
the shit!' she counters Jerry's earlier accusation.

'We—I—want gentleness, Shell,' Jerry hears himself say. 'At
least sometimes.' He thinks: a gentleness that will flower from
the relentless wounds of cruelty. And death. The ultimate
cruelty.

Shell laughs harshly. 'Gentleness!' she yells at him. 'Man,
you are so fucked up! Man, you don't even know it! Man, if
you haven't learned from all you've seen!'

'Especially after that,' Jerry says.

Shell's voice breaks: 'Wow!' She touches her head as if re-
orienting herself. 'Wow!—and so we fucking got to each
other. But we're still the angels,' she tries frantically to dissipate
the barbarous tension. 'That's all it was,' she says firmly. But
the desolation grows. 'Now we're like closer, man. Don't you
see?' Waves of isolation engulf her. She looks imploringly at
Cob; up the stairs at Manny. She faces Jerry. 'Like we're really
close,' she insists. 'We know where each is at, and we can hassle
it. We've faced the worst shit. Like Manny knows . . .'

Manny says: 'I didn't want to know, Shell.'

'We're *together*!' Shell insists. 'None of us will ever, ever
cry again! The four fucking angels!' Urgently she looks for her
suede bag, finds it on the floor. She brings out a joint of grass.
She lights it with determinedly steady fingers. She inhales urgently. Moving quickly to him—anxious to complete the binding gesture, the meaning of the cigarette—she holds it to Cob.

Cob doesn't take it. She extends it closer to him. Still he
doesn't move. She holds it to his lips. 'Do it, man,' she almost
pleads. 'We're the four angels. Please . . .'

Cob moves away from her. Then: the sound of the door. He's gone. Alone.

Shell closes her eyes. Quickly, she opens them determinedly. Manny is coming down the stairs, as if to leave too.

Shell intercepts him, holds the joint urgently to him. 'Manny?'

He stares down at it. Alone, confused, he frowns. He shakes his head; he moves away from her; he stands undecided by the door.

Shell moves swiftly up the stairs, to Jerry. 'Jerry . . .' She holds the joint to him.

Jerry doesn't take it.

She extends the joint closer to him. 'Please!'

Jerry reaches for it, takes it, inhales from it. Gently, he returns it to her.

Shell holds it, frowns. Then she says quietly: 'I proved . . . *I* didn't cry.'

Suddenly she moves away from Jerry, past Manny, out the door.

Manny sighs: 'I don't know where to go now.' Slowly he leaves the house.

Jerry remains on the stairs looking into the vast darkness.

Outside. Shell runs down the steps. Quickly she's in her car. She starts it. It dies. 'God-fucking-damn!' she yells angrily. She starts it again. With a vicious jerk, it lunges forward. She drives urgently into the freeway along the scorching, dry Texas night.

She reaches the crossroads, turns. Trees are black, like jagged paper silhouettes. And now she's on the levee. She drives recklessly along the dirt road, dust stirred angrily. She's left the few scattered cars behind her. She stops abruptly.

The river.

She gets out of the car. She stares at the small sandy island on the water—where they built their dazzling sand castle that joyous afternoon—and then destroyed it. Where they stood that strange night, naked, like sentinels guarding their worlds.

Where so much passed, silently, between them.

She stares at the black river, the trees, the sand. She removes her shoes. She wades across the water in her torn dress, her flesh welcoming the cool water.

She stands on the island. Their island. She looks to one side, to the other. Remembering how they stood, those magic moments. Apart. But close. Close in the currents of the drugged world. She looks down at the sand, moist. Remembers: the castle.

She stands alone on this island on the dark, deserted river.

Suddenly, like a terrified child, she lies on the sand. She nestles her face against it. It's the sand's moisture, she tells herself, it isn't tears.